The

Leipzig
Vampire

YEARLING BOOKS/YOUNG YEARLINGS/YEARLING CLASSICS are designed especially to entertain and enlighten young people. Patricia Reilly Giff, consultant to this series, received the bachelor's degree from Marymount College. She holds the master's degree in history from St. John's University, and a Professional Diploma in Reading from Hofstra University. She was a teacher and reading consultant for many years, and is the author of numerous books for young readers.

For a complete listing of all Yearling titles, write to
Dell Readers Service, P.O. Box 1045,
South Holland, IL 60473.

MOSTLY GHOSTS

The
Leipzig
Vampire

by Mary Anderson

A YEARLING BOOK

Published by
Dell Publishing
a division of
Bantam Doubleday Dell Publishing Group, Inc.
666 Fifth Avenue
New York, New York 10103

The trademark Yearling® is registered in the U.S. Patent and Trademark Office.

ISBN: 0-440-44719-4

Printed in the United States of America

October 1987

10   9   8   7   6   5   4   3

CW

Chapter One

JAMIE ENTERED THE HOUSE, SNIFFING THE AIR DISAPPROVINGLY. "What's that strange smell?"

"When referring to food," his mother replied, "the proper word is *aroma*."

Jamie did not agree. "It's a smell—a *rotten* one."

"It's actually garlic," explained his father. "Your mom just read a fascinating book called *Garlic Can Change Your Life*, so she's giving it a try. Judging from the *aroma*, I suspect she put some in every course—with the possible exception of our dessert, I hope."

Jamie glanced at his twin sister, Amy, who was also frowning. They both agreed the smell was awful.

"I don't want my life changed," Amy said. "I thought we were having burgers. I had my mouth all set for burgers."

Mrs. Ferguson wiped her hands on a dish towel. "Bet-

1

ter get your mouth set for something completely new and different," she said. "Tonight's dinner is going to be special. Your dad has invited a new colleague from the university to join us."

The twins were accustomed to having last-minute guests for dinner, but usually their mother did not make such a fuss. In fact, they had entertained so many Monroe professors at their dinner table, Jamie often referred to their dining room as "the annex" of the university.

"What's so special about this guest?" Amy asked, "and why can't he eat burgers?"

"Dr. Gustav Manheim is an eminent scientist from Germany," Mr. Ferguson explained. "Maybe your mom feels he's above burgers."

Jamie suddenly grew interested. "A scientist? What's his specialty, Dad?"

"It's hard to say; he has so many. Dr. Manheim is a biochemist and a hematologist, but he also has a degree in zoology, so what would you say that makes him?"

"Very educated," said Jamie.

"Very old," said Amy.

"Very impressive," added Mrs. Ferguson.

"Yes, he's all of that," Mr. Ferguson said, "and very learned as well. Dr. Manheim is giving a series of graduate seminars at Monroe in conjunction with his latest paper on genetic diseases."

Amy groaned. She absolutely hated fusty, dreary academic discussions over dinner—especially when the dinner wasn't burgers. As was his habit, Jamie would grab the opportunity to show off his smarts! Somehow, he

seemed always to know at least a little bit about everything, so he would probably have something intelligent
to say even about biochemistry!

It was all so predictable, Amy thought; she needn't
bother to use her psychic powers to know the outcome of
this evening: Their guest would quickly realize that Jamie
was the brilliant one and Amy was not.

Yes, Jamie was looking forward to meeting their guest.
He liked impressing people with his superior intelligence.
Lately, however, he had begun to feel that perhaps brains
alone weren't everything. Ever since he'd discovered that
his sister had psychic ability, Jamie wondered if he wasn't
missing out on something. After all, Amy was the one
who had seen visions of their ancestor, Jebediah Aloysious
Tredwell. *She* was the one the ghost had spoken with,
not *him*. Somehow, a thing like that could make a superior person feel awfully *inferior*.

All the more reason to impress Dr. Manheim, Jamie
reasoned. Besides, he was genuinely interested in dis-
cussing the doctor's specialties. Jamie knew he would
have to make a decision about his own career someday,
and twelve seemed an appropriate age to begin.

Most recently Jamie had considered becoming a history
professor like his father, but he'd already abandoned that
idea. His mind was too active to be confined to events of
the past when the future seemed far more challenging.
But what field would best benefit from his academic
gifts? he wondered. Medicine? Science? Business?

"Has everyone checked out?" asked Mrs. Ferguson,

looking frazzled. "Not a soul has offered to help, and the table hasn't been set yet."

"Sorry, Miriam," said her husband. "Which glasses are we using?"

"Water and wine, I think."

"No wine for me, Mom," Jamie joked. "I have to keep my wits about me."

"Very funny, young man. Please take out the soup tureen and the blue-and-white china. Amy, get the silver candlesticks."

Amy opened the china closet. "You're really doing things up big tonight."

The Fergusons' blue-and-white china had been in the family for centuries. The silver candlesticks had been made by Paul Revere, and the famous patriot himself had presented them to Lieutenant Colonel Tredwell sometime after the Revolution. They were highly prized and used only on special occasions.

Mr. Ferguson held up a crystal goblet, checking it for smudge marks. "Dr. Manheim is a very special guest," he said. "He's considered one of the finest minds in Europe, so we're fortunate he accepted the offer to lecture at Monroe. He's actually somewhat of a recluse; he rarely gives interviews and keeps his research top secret."

"What kind of research?" asked Amy.

"Don't be dense," said Jamie. "Dad just said it was secret, so how would he know?"

Amy hadn't asked out of mere curiosity. She had just received one of her peculiar psychic twinges and somehow knew it pertained to Dr. Manheim. Suddenly she felt uneasy.

Amy was not entirely comfortable about having psychic abilities. She had sworn her brother to secrecy—no one was to know about her power; but she still was not certain he would keep his word. After all, forever is a long time and Amy wanted her secret kept forever. So far Jamie had not told a soul, but she was not sure how long that would last.

Very often Amy felt as if she were balancing precariously between safe, predictable reality and the unsettling unnerving world of her psychic visions, and she disliked that feeling. The only pleasant thing had been her occasional meetings with Jebediah Tredwell, her ancestor. Meeting a ghost might have frightened some people, but Amy considered him a friend—not unlike the imaginary friends she had conjured up for herself when she was little. Unfortunately, Jebediah's spirit had not returned.

"That garlic smell is getting stronger," Jamie complained. "Can't you spritz some air spray in the kitchen?"

Mrs. Ferguson finished folding the linen napkins. "I guess my first course is ready. I hope Dr. Manheim doesn't arrive late. I've timed everything for eight o'clock."

"Manheim is a perfectionist," said Mr. Ferguson, "so I'm sure he'll be prompt. By the way, Miriam, don't be insulted if he doesn't shake hands—he never does. And he might wear his white gloves to the dinner table."

"Why?" asked his wife. "Is one of his many professions that of a *butler*?"

"I'm not sure why, but I didn't think it polite to ask. I

suspect he was injured or burned during the war. Anyway, I've never seen him without his white gloves."

Jamie began reconsidering his career choices again. "Maybe he was mangled by one of his bestial zoological specimens. Or disfigured while creating a demonic Dr. Hyde biochemical compound," he added dramatically. "Supposedly safe professions can sometimes be the most dangerous."

Amy looked exasperated. "Dad, Jamie's career talk is driving me crazy. Last week he eliminated aviation, the law, and oceanography. Nothing seems good enough for him!"

Mr. Ferguson set down the last china plate. "No one can be overprepared for the future, Amy, so let your brother explore his options. And let Jamie talk with Dr. Manheim if he likes."

"I don't care who he talks to," she protested.

"Oh really? Then why is it that whenever we have guests who interest Jamie, I can hear rumblings underneath the table—as if you were bashing your feet against your brother's knees?"

"Right, she *always* does that, Dad. Intelligent conversation is above her head."

"It is not," Amy argued, "it's just boring."

"Well, kindly be bored with your *brain*, not your feet, young lady."

"Okay, Dad." Amy sulked, and grew silent. Something about the upcoming dinner was making her more and more uneasy. Amy felt a wave of psychic presentiment, which she often experienced before an unpleasant

6

occurrence, and she was convinced it was connected with Dr. Manheim. Suddenly she did not want to meet him. "Do I have to stay for dinner, Dad? I think I'm getting a headache."

"Who're you kidding?" asked Jamie. "You just don't want to eat an all-garlic dinner. But if I have to stay and eat it, you do too!"

"Don't let your mother hear you talk like that," warned Mr. Ferguson. "She has no sense of humor concerning her culinary experiments."

The prospect of an all-garlic dinner was not a pleasant one, but that's not what bothered Amy. It was meeting Dr. Manheim. Why? she wondered. Why should she feel so apprehensive? Amy had a strange psychic sense that the doctor wasn't at all what he pretended to be.

Before Amy could dwell on the thought further, the door bell rang.

Chapter Two

"I'LL GET IT," SAID JAMIE, HURRYING INTO THE LIVING ROOM.

As he opened the front door Jamie was startled to see the stately figure in the doorway. Dr. Manheim was much taller than Jamie had expected—over six feet. He was obviously quite old, yet he stood stiffly erect, almost like a statue. He definitely made an impression. Dressed entirely in black, except for a starched white shirt and white kid gloves, he had a strong, angular face and a long white mustache which flowed beneath his aquiline nose and arched nostrils. Wavy white hair fell over the back of his black woolen cape. He looked, Jamie thought, more like an elderly member of a rock group than an eminent scientist.

The doctor nodded but did not smile. "Good evening."

"Hi there," Jamie said brightly, extending his hand. The doctor refused it. Instead he removed his floppy black felt hat, tipped it, and made a graceful bow. Then he swirled his cape from around his shoulders and rested it across his arm.

Mr. Ferguson came to the door. "Come in, Dr. Manheim. It's an honor to have you here."

"The honor is all mine," he replied.

As the old man entered the living room a chill raced through Amy's body. She stared at Dr. Manheim's face; it seemed to have a strange unearthly quality. His eyes were almost black, and his skin had a sickly pallor. Even his lips were pale, as if all the color had been drained from his body. He was so thin that the flesh was pulled taut around his face, as if covering a skull.

As Amy took the doctor's cape and hat she felt another cold sensation. The fabric seemed clammy; the musty odor of damp earth was embedded within the fibers. Watching the old man sit down on the sofa, Amy could almost hear the dry, brittle bones crackling underneath his black suit.

"It was most kind of you to invite me to your home, Professor Ferguson. Often I tend to feel somewhat of a stranger in a strange land."

Jamie noted the doctor's charming European accent. "You've never been here in the States before?" he asked.

"No, I have not. Although many of my kind have come before me."

What a funny expression, Jamie thought. "Your *kind*? Oh, you mean your relatives."

"I mean my ancestors. In one way or another we Manheims have explored the globe."

Mrs. Ferguson entered the room and reached out her hand in greeting. Once again Dr. Manheim refused to extend his. Instead he stood up and bowed. "Forgive what you must surely consider my rudeness," he said, "but I have an aversion to personal contact. A family idiosyncrasy which I beg you to indulge."

"That's quite all right," she said, smiling. "I hope you've brought your appetite with you, Doctor. Dinner's almost ready."

"My appetite is shamefully slight, but your invitation is nonetheless appreciated."

"Oh, you'll love Miriam's cooking," said Mr. Ferguson. "I guess you don't get too many home-cooked meals over at the Monroe Arms."

"I no longer reside there," the doctor said. "I have recently found a house just outside of town which suits my needs quite admirably."

"That's nice," said Mrs. Ferguson. "Where is it?"

"North of Fairview Terrace and just a bit beyond Chestnut Drive."

"That's impossible," said Jamie. "There's nothing out there but the old graveyard."

"And the abandoned Brewster place," his father added, "but that's far too run-down to be habitable."

Dr. Manheim leaned back on the sofa. "You Americans are accustomed to far too many luxuries," he said with disdain. "I, on the other hand, am not. The old Brewster place, as you call it, is quite habitable. What's more important, it has seclusion, which is imperative to my work. It's necessary I continue my experiments during my stay here."

Mrs. Ferguson seemed surprised. The old Brewster place had not been lived in for ages! But maybe a new paint job, crisp curtains, and slipcovers, plus a deft woman's touch, could make it homey again. "I'm afraid it'll take your wife a while to put that place in order," she said. "If she needs any assistance, I'd be glad to help."

"I have no wife," Dr. Manheim said solemnly.

"Don't you have any family with you?" Jamie asked.

The doctor grew thoughtful, as if considering the question. "Family? In a manner of speaking. I have not come to this country alone. Two have come with me."

Mr. Ferguson offered the doctor a canapé, which he politely refused. "I had no idea you planned to conduct experiments while you're here."

"Oh, yes, my work is far too vital to be interrupted for any length of time. Many lives may hang in the balance."

"Sounds fascinating," Jamie said. "Can't you tell us anything about your project?"

Dr. Manheim shrugged. "I'm afraid you'd find my theories most unorthodox, young man. To my mind, the medical profession is steeped in archaic superstition which makes it impossible to initiate significant breakthroughs within the established community."

Mr. Ferguson nodded in agreement. "You've always been considered a renegade scientist, haven't you, Doctor? I hope you don't mind me saying that."

"It's absolute fact," Dr. Manheim agreed. "In Leipzig there are very few research labs still at my disposal. Therefore, I've been forced to create my own laboratories."

Jamie was impressed. "Is your work that controversial?"

"This is not unusual," the doctor replied. "Controversy has always plagued truly innovative thought. Lister, Pasteur, Gallie, Carswell, Bremer—they were all considered either mad, incompetent, or egomaniacal." Dr. Manheim began rubbing his gloved hands together nervously. "Working in seclusion is the only way to protect oneself from the prying eyes of the ignorant and uninformed. Medical breakthroughs are never created by committees in boardrooms under the scrutiny of trustees. It is always one man—alone—traveling through the darkness toward the light. Always."

Jamie listened to the doctor with admiration. The field of investigative medicine was suddenly sounding terrifically challenging. Experimental scientists were actually explorers who traveled through totally unknown territory. Superhonchos who often got things named after them— not only diseases, milk, and mouthwashes, but hospitals, buildings, and *awards*. Jamie's mind raced toward a possible future date when someone might receive the Jamie Ferguson Medal for Distinguished Scientific Achievement. Yes, science was definitely a field to consider.

But how about the money? he wondered. It was all very well to be noble, but he wouldn't mind being rich too. "Do you have trouble finding funds for your projects?" he asked. "I mean, since you refuse to tell anyone what you're doing."

"There are many who accept my terms," the doctor replied. "Many private organizations and foundations feel medical progress takes precedence over publicity. Such people prefer to remain anonymous."

12

Jamie got the point. "Sure, science can be a great tax shelter—and a terrific tax write-off."

"Excuse my son," Mr. Ferguson said "Jamie is considering possible career choices, and I think yours seems very intriguing at the moment."

Dr. Manheim stared at Jamie with piercing black eyes. "Do not enter this field unless you are prepared to suffer," he warned. "Science will accept nothing less than total commitment. It will bend you to its will and perhaps leave you disillusioned. Often it will sap your strength and energy and make you go beyond your own endurance, seeking the solutions you know exist somewhere beyond your grasp. If science is your true interest, Jamie, you must be prepared to become obsessed with its demands. No door will open easily."

Jamie reconsidered the prospect. "I was certainly hoping for a nine-to-five deal."

The Fergusons chuckled, but Dr. Manheim saw no humor in Jamie's answer. "This is not the case with science," he said sternly. "I have found some nights to be long as an eternity. Luckily, I have learned to make the night my ally—and the creatures of the night my friends."

Amy sat silently, deliberately averting her eyes from the guest. His presence made her feel uncomfortable and his face frightened her.

"I understand you're also a zoologist," said Mrs. Ferguson, "so I'm sure *all* living creatures are of interest to you, Doctor."

"True," he said, nodding. "But nocturnal creatures

13

harbor many secrets medical science has yet to unlock. The night itself holds many mysteries," he added, staring thoughtfully into space.

Amy shuddered. Dr. Manheim's remark had brought a disturbing image to her mind. She envisioned the strange old man stalking through the graveyard in the moonlight. Behind him was a female figure draped in a gauzy white gown. Overhead, winged creatures were crying as they flew through the inky sky.

Mrs. Ferguson glanced at her daughter. "What's wrong, Amy, don't you feel well?"

Amy quickly shook the image from her mind. "I think I'm a little dizzy, Mom."

"That must be hunger," said her mother. "We'd better begin dinner."

"Not just yet," said Mr. Ferguson, taking his camera from the coffee table. "I need a picture for our scrapbook. All eminent visitors wind up in the Ferguson scrapbook," he explained, aiming the camera toward Dr. Manheim.

Just as the flashbulb was about to pop, the doctor jumped up and quickly turned his head. "Please, I beg your indulgence," he said emphatically. "My eyes are too weak for such bright light. A genetic problem, you understand."

Embarrassed, Mr. Ferguson quickly put down the camera. "Yes, of course. I'm terribly sorry."

Noticing that he'd startled everyone, Dr. Manheim now spoke in a calm voice: "Think nothing of it. I regret I cannot oblige."

Amy's psychic energies kept flowing. She knew the

14

doctor had lied. There was some other reason why he had refused to pose for the camera. But what was it?

As everyone rose to enter the dining room the clock above the mirrored mantel struck eight. Hearing it chime, Dr. Manheim lowered his head, then nervously walked toward the corner of the room. He didn't enter the dining room through the center door but went through the kitchen instead. "Forgive my curiosity," he said, "but I am fascinated by all your modern American appliances."

Mrs. Ferguson was delighted. "I'd love to give you a tour," she said, and proudly pointed out her new microwave oven.

Amy watched as the doctor pretended interest. *Another lie*. Dr. Manheim had deliberately avoided walking past the mirror. Why?

Amy's psychic instincts confirmed that there was something secretive and sinister about the old man. Approaching the dinner table, she received another image of creatures flying through the graveyard. Blood was trickling down their viciously sharp teeth.

"Don't stand in a daze, Amy," her mother whispered. "Help Dr. Manheim with his chair."

Amy leaned over and pulled out a chair for the guest.

Dr. Manheim bowed graciously, then looked up and smiled. "Thank you, my dear."

It was then that Amy noticed his teeth. She had never seen an old man with such white teeth. Very white and very *sharp*.

Chapter Three

MRS. FERGUSON PLACED A TUREEN ON THE TABLE. "MUSHROOM garlic soup," she said, lifting the lid to reveal the steaming soup.

As she ladled the soup into his bowl, Dr. Manheim cringed. "A thousand apologies, dear lady, but I have an allergy to bulbous plants."

"Really? Oh dear, garlic is a main feature of this meal. Can I whip you up an omelet or something else instead?"

"Your gracious company is food enough. Please forgive my abstinence."

Jamie swished the soup around in his bowl, wishing he had the same excuse. Reluctantly he tasted it. To his surprise, it wasn't bad. Sprinkled with crumbled bread sticks, it was actually good.

Dr. Manheim sipped his wine as his hosts began the

meal. Amy only pretended to eat, as her disturbing vision had ruined her appetite.

The second course was prawns in garlic sauce. To Jamie's amazement, that wasn't bad either.

"I'm looking forward to your seminars," Mr. Ferguson said. "Luckily, they're all at night, so I can attend them."

"I *always* lecture at night," the doctor explained. "I do everything at night."

Mr. Ferguson began carving the roast beef his wife had placed on the table. As the knife cut through the meat, red juice burst from the center.

"I hope you like your meat rare," he said, filling the doctor's plate.

Dr. Manheim's eyes brightened as the plate was placed before him. Eagerly he lifted his soupspoon to sip the bloody juices. "Perfection," he declared. "Most Americans tend to cremate their meat, which I consider disgraceful."

Amy watched in disgust as a tiny trickle of blood ran down the doctor's white teeth and onto his chin. He quickly wiped it away with his napkin.

"I like rare meat too," Mr. Ferguson said.

Mrs. Ferguson was relieved. Finally her guest had approved of some part of the meal. She made a mental note never to serve garlic again without checking beforehand!

Dr. Manheim declined the broccoli in garlic sauce and the garlic potatoes au gratin. "I am more than satisfied with the roast and wine," he explained. Amy noticed that after he had eaten a small amount, a hint of color entered his cheeks.

Dr. Manheim held up the crystal goblet in his gloved hand, admiring the design. "Such beautiful crystal. Is it Austrian?"

"Yes," said Mrs. Ferguson. "It's a Tredwell heirloom. These goblets have been in my family since the eighteenth century."

The doctor seemed startled. "Tredwell?" he asked. "Under what circumstance are you aware of that name?"

"That's Miriam's maiden name," explained Mr. Ferguson. "The Tredwells and the Cartwrights practically founded the town of Monroe."

"And Alexander Cartwright founded our school too," Jamie explained. "It's called Hillcrest Academy."

Dr. Manheim's hand trembled as he set down the goblet abruptly.

"Is something wrong?" asked Mrs. Ferguson.

"No, dear lady. Unusual, that is all. Are you familiar with Jung's theory of synchronicity?"

"Why, yes," she said. "It's a meaningful coincidence far beyond the laws of probability."

"Exactly. What would you say if I told you my ancestors were acquainted with *both* the Tredwells and the Cartwrights?"

"That certainly *is* a coincidence," Jamie said.

"Most assuredly," said the doctor. "In past centuries their paths crossed on more than one occasion."

"I'm not surprised," said Mr. Ferguson. "One of Miriam's ancestors, Jebediah Tredwell, was quite a world traveler. After he'd served in the Revolutionary War, he became a wealthy merchant, and I'm sure he often vis-

18

ited Leipzig. It just proves the world is a small place. That's what I always tell my history students. Customs may differ from country to country, but people are basically the same."

"I don't agree," the doctor said vehemently. "History has proved that the human race is prejudiced against all those who are different. They either *shun* them or pursue them like animals, and they cringe in fear and ignorance. Yes, ignorance is the cornerstone of *all* societies. In many respects we're no more enlightened than those who lived in the Middle Ages, a time when people were burned alive or impaled on stakes."

"That's a harsh view of mankind," said Mrs. Ferguson, "though I suppose we all have a dark side to our nature."

Dr. Manheim nodded knowingly. "Yes, the human psyche is indeed dark and mysterious."

Mrs. Ferguson tried to lighten the conversation. "Before we all get too somber, I suggest we have dessert. Amy, would you please bring it in?"

Deep into her psychic thoughts, Amy hadn't heard her mother. She now knew why Dr. Manheim frightened her. His presence in Monroe meant danger for everyone. Staring into his black eyes, she saw a disturbing vision of darkness, nocturnal creatures, and *death*.

"Amy, would you bring in the cake, dear?"

Amy blinked, then pushed her chair from the table.

"Listen," Jamie mumbled, "don't poke your filthy fingers in the frosting."

Her brother's sappy statement brought Amy back to reality. She told herself that she hadn't had a psychic vision. Because Dr. Manheim was creepy-looking and strange, her imagination had run wild. After all, no one else was scared of him. No one even seemed to think he was peculiar.

Relieved now, she entered the kitchen and placed her mother's chocolate cheese cake on a china platter, then put the cake dishes on a tray. There was nothing to be concerned about, she told herself. *Nothing.*

Amy noticed that the cake server was missing, so she went into the pantry to find it. As she opened the cupboard door a golden glow filled the alcove. Within seconds the illuminating energy had formed itself into a shape. And that shape gradually transformed itself into the figure of her ancestor, Lieutenant Colonel Jebediah Aloysious Tredwell. She could see him standing by the cupboard door, wearing the uniform of the colonial revolutionists and looking exactly as he had the last time she had seen him.

"Jeb, is it really you?" she whispered. "I never thought I'd see your ghost again."

"Spirit," he said, correcting her. "You seem sincerely surprised, Cousin. Did I not tell you we would meet again?"

"But I've looked for you lots of times. I thought maybe my psychic powers were gone. Jamie said that seeing your spirit might just be a flash in the pan—a fluke."

Indignantly Jebediah placed his hands on his hips. "I cannot comprehend such verbiage. Let me assure you, child, your psychic gifts are intact. If this were not the case, we could not have this conversation. Logic attests to that."

20

Amy shook her head. "I don't know. Jamie is the *logical* one, but he can't see or hear you. What sense does that make?"

"All things within the universe make sense," Jebediah said with conviction. "You may console yourself in that fact. But hear me, child; I am not composed of idle breath. I come here with a purpose. Although my life on earth is done, your life and mine shall be eternally entwined. You have an uneasiness of spirit which distresses me, for my soul shares this very same concern."

"It does?"

"Indeed so. Hark ye now, a word in your ear. My time here is brief, so attend me. Trust your instincts, Cousin; they shall not betray you."

"My instincts tell me something *creepy* is going on. I don't like our guest, Dr. Manheim. I think he's evil. In fact, I think he looks like the devil."

"Nay, child. 'Tis the devil who is blamed for more than his due. I have observed the one of whom you speak, and have been acquainted with others of his kind."

"His *kind*? Oh, you mean his ancestors. Yes, Dr. Manheim said his ancestors knew some of your relatives. Tell me about him, Jebediah. Is he really evil? I have this awful feeling something terrible will happen if he stays in Monroe."

"Calm yourself, child. Would that I had leave to illuminate the situation, but as you know, I cannot alter the present without grave risk to my own spirit. This much I can attest to: The man who dines with you this evening may most assuredly be involved in evil intrigue. In the

21

circuit of fortune's wheel you and your brother may be drawn into his affairs. I charge you, take care."

"But *how*?" Amy said pleadingly. "What awful things might happen, Jeb? I keep seeing images of ugly creatures and a strange woman wandering through the graveyard. What's it mean?"

"It means you must be on your guard; I would take my book oath on it. There are things within the universe many cannot comprehend and many more deny, yet this does not alter their existence one whit. Would that I could say more." Jebediah's spirit slowly began to fade. "Take care, Cousin. Take care!" Jebediah vanished as suddenly as he had appeared.

"What's holding up dessert?" asked Jamie, hurrying into the pantry. "You're missing some great conversation, Amy. Old Dr. Manheim is a real genius."

"I think he's a real creep," she said. "He's up to something *evil*, and our lives may be in danger."

Jamie stared at his sister. "Are you bonkers, or have you been sipping Mom's cooking sherry?"

"It's *true*, Jamie. That old man isn't what he seems to be. Did you notice the way he behaved at the dinner table—the way he ate the roast?"

"Sure, he's an old man and he dribbled a little. So what? It's probably because he has to wear gloves when he eats."

"*Why* does he wear gloves? There's something strange about his hands, that's why."

Jamie sighed. "An idiot could've figured that out! I guess that explains how *you* could arrive at that amazing

22

conclusion. Wearing gloves doesn't make a person evil; only different."

"Jebediah agrees with me," Amy said smugly. "He thinks there's something dangerous about Dr. Manheim too!"

"*Jeb*? What's he got to do with this?"

"I saw his spirit again."

"When?"

"Just a minute ago, right here in the pantry. Jeb came to warn me about Dr. Manheim. I've been getting scary visions about him all evening."

"Boy, are you *prejudiced*, Amy. That's exactly what the doctor was talking about earlier. Just because a guy dresses strangely, eats funny, and has to wear gloves, you consider him a *creep*. Well, I'll tell you something. Manheim has a brilliant mind, but that's something you wouldn't know about."

At that point Mr. Ferguson walked into the kitchen. "I'm here to investigate the case of the missing cheesecake," he explained, "which has led to the mystery of the missing twins. What's going on in here?"

"Sorry, Dad," Amy said. "I couldn't find the cake server. I'll plug in the coffeepot, then I'll be out in a second."

"Just for the record, Dad," said Jamie, "what do *you* think of Dr. Manheim?"

"I think he's an innovative scientist. I also think he's a bit eccentric. Why do you ask?"

"Because Amy think he's—"

23

"Much too skinny," she interrupted. "Maybe this cheese-cake will fatten him up."

Several hours after the Fergusons had gone to bed, they were awakened by a strange sound that seemed to come from somewhere in the woods behind the house.

Mrs. Ferguson switched on the lamp by the night table. "Did you hear that, Richard?" she asked.

Her husband tossed restlessly. "How could I help it?"

"Well, what do you think it is? It sounds like some poor animal caught in a trap."

"It must be Barney Ogilvy's sheepdog. Sometimes Barney lets him out at night. You know how Wiffenpoof loves to prowl."

"Prowl, yes; but I never heard Wiffenpoof scream like a banshee!"

"There's a first time for everything, Miriam; go back to sleep."

As Miriam Ferguson slipped back under the covers, the strange, unearthly cry pierced the air again. It sounded absolutely nothing like Wiffenpoof, she thought to herself. Then she yawned, rolled over, and went back to sleep.

Chapter Four

THE NEXT MORNING JEMIMA APTHORP, HEADMISTRESS OF HILL-crest Academy, was standing by the main staircase as the students entered the school.

"David Toshito," she said sharply, "kindly remove those ridiculous creatures from your jacket pocket. I'm quite aware Halloween is a few days away, but you can't play those silly pranks in school."

David pulled out the collection of wriggly rubber rats, spiders, and bats hanging from his pocket. "I planned to keep them in my desk," he explained.

Miss Apthorp looked skeptical. "Indeed? I'm sure eventually they'd wiggle their way into our cloakroom and bathrooms, David. So if you don't mind, I'll keep them in *my* desk until school is over."

The twins watched as Miss Apthorp slipped the rubber creatures into her own pocket. "Too bad, David," said

25

Jamie, "but you can't get anything past old Appy's eagle eye. I tried the same trick last year and she caught me. I guess Miss A. is too old to really enjoy Halloween."

David shrugged. "I don't care, as long as I get my stuff back before we celebrate the Night Parade of One Hundred Demons."

"What's that?" asked Amy.

"It's a Japanese ceremony that's a lot like Halloween. My uncle still does it for us kids. Once a year we all get together to tell ghost stories. One hundred candles are lit, and as each story is told a candle is blown out. When all one hundred stories have been told, ghosts are supposed to appear."

"No kidding, does it work?" Jamie asked.

"Who knows? I always fall asleep after the first few stories."

"You should invite Amy to that ceremony," Jamie said teasingly. "She knows a ghost personally." Jamie was still mad at his sister for what she'd said about Dr. Manheim the night before. He knew that the slightest suggestion he might reveal her psychic powers always made Amy a nervous wreck.

Amy flashed her brother a filthy look. "Don't pay attention to anything Jamie says, David. He's practicing for his upcoming career as an idiot."

"For which you don't need any practice," Jamie shot back. "You're so good at that already."

Miss Apthorp surveyed the main hall for stragglers late for their classes. "Amy and Jamie Ferguson, hurry along to English class."

26

Amy hated the idea of having English first thing in the morning. All her marks were poor, but English was usually her worst subject. Her teacher, Mrs. Eliot, was rarely understanding about Amy's poor grades because Jamie did so well in her class.

Amy was always annoyed by people who treated twins as *clones*. After all, they were separate individuals. Unfortunately, Jamie had all the practical gifts and she had all the peculiar ones—but she still felt she'd been right about Dr. Manheim. Amy was certain Jebediah had materialized to warn her of the danger the old man brought to Monroe, and she had yet to figure out what the danger might be.

The twins hurried to their seats as Mrs. Eliot called the class to order. "I'm sure it's no news to anyone that Halloween is coming soon," she announced. "What is news is that this year the township is sponsoring a special All Hallows' Eve celebration outdoors in Winchester Field. All parents and children are invited to join in a costume competition; the prizewinner will receive twenty-five dollars."

The entire class was thrilled with the idea.

"In addition," said Mrs. Eliot, "I've decided to have my own competition as part of the festivities. I'd like each of you to write a ghost story, and the best submission will also receive a prize."

"Twenty-five dollars?" asked Henry Plimpton hopefully.

"No, a book of poetry."

The class groaned.

"That's no fun," said Melissa Petronio. "If we write

27

scary stories, we should receive an *appropriate* prize, not poetry."

Mrs. Eliot smiled. "Your point is well taken, Melissa; but a book of poetry *is* appropriate. Perhaps you don't realize that poetry and scary tales are often synonymous. Let me tell you a story about two very famous nineteenth-century poets, Lord Byron and Percy Bysshe Shelley. Once Byron rented a house near Geneva. It was called the Villa Diodati. Shelley and his young wife, Mary, were living in an adjoining house and the couple spent many evenings in Byron's company at the Villa Diodati. They would read one another German ghost stories. Then Byron and Shelley decided they would have a little competition, similar to the one I've proposed. They would each write their own ghost story, to see which would be most frightening. And that is how the famous novel *Frankenstein* came to be written. Mary Shelley was the woman who breathed life into the monster Frankenstein created, and she was barely twenty years old at the time."

"I'll bet she won the prize," said Henry. "How'd those two guys do?"

"Not badly. After all, they were both famous poets. Let me read you part of a poem Byron wrote that illustrates that fact." Mrs. Eliot opened her book, cleared her throat, and began:

" 'But first on earth, as Vampyre sent,
Thy corpse shall from its tomb be rent;
Then ghastly haunt thy native place,
And suck the blood of all thy race;

28

There from thy daughter, sister, wife,
At midnight drain the stream of life.' "

"Gross out," said Henry. "Guys were writing stuff like that hundreds of years ago?"

"Certainly," said Mrs. Eliot. "Monsters didn't originate in horror movies, you know. They're products of fertile creative minds. So let's see how fertile you children can be. Dig into that creative soil and unearth some marvelous stories for me. The winner will get this book which includes the full text of the poem that I've just read from; it's called *The Giaour*."

Jamie grew excited. Competitions always got his adrenaline flowing. He had not realized that *Frankenstein* had been the product of a *contest*. Maybe, if he wrote a good enough story, *his* might be published too! What should it be about? he wondered. Ghouls? Goblins? Witches?

"A *vampire*," Amy whispered. She had leaned across Jamie's desk and was tugging on his arm. "I just figured it out. That's what Jebediah was trying to tell us. That's what my psychic vision meant."

"*What?*"

"He's a *vampire*, Jamie. Dr. Manheim is a vampire!"

Mrs. Eliot tapped her desk with a pencil. "Amy, if you have something to say, perhaps you'd like to share it with the entire class?"

Jamie giggled. "Yeah, tell the class what you just told me," he whispered.

Amy felt ridiculous. "I'm sorry, Mrs. Eliot. It was something personal, between me and Jamie."

29

"That's right," Jamie said facetiously. "It was about our dinner guest last night."

"Then we don't need to hear it, do we?" Mrs. Eliot said sternly.

Amy blushed. "No, ma'am."

"Very well. Now, class, I'd like you to spend the next few minutes thinking over possible story ideas. Remember, the scarier the better. Get those creative juices flowing!"

Amy glared at her brother as he began writing feverishly. For a person with supposed intelligence, he was awfully stupid. *Why* didn't he believe her? It had come to Amy in a flash of recognition when Mrs. Eliot had begun reading the poem: Her psychic premonition was really a vision of Dr. Manheim on the prowl for *blood*.

Amy remembered the warning Jebediah had given her. She and Jamie *were* in danger! But how could she convince her brother of that? She began doodling in her notebook, too preoccupied to write.

Jamie sat at the corner desk and stared out the window. Gray storm clouds had been threatening rain all morning. He was thinking now of possible story ideas. Witches were too corny. What about a slime monster who lived at the bottom of a lake and oozed green fungus all over fishermen? Terrific.

Jamie was into the second paragraph of his story when Miss Apthorp rushed into the room looking extremely upset. "Excuse me, class, but I must speak with Mrs. Eliot."

The two women stood at the front of the room talking

quietly. Pretty soon Mrs. Eliot also looked extremely upset.

Amy sensed something really serious had happened.

"Attention, class," said Mrs. Eliot. "Miss Apthorp has just told me something very distressing. As you know, I'm in charge of the exhibits in the library, and it seems a theft has just been discovered. Do any of you children know who might have vandalized the display case?"

Students glanced at one another, but no one seemed to know what Mrs. Eliot was talking about.

The display case stood in a corner of the library, and Mrs. Eliot usually changed the exhibits each month. Alexander Cartwright, the founder of the school, had a vast collection of rare manuscripts and antique volumes which he had purchased during his world travels. The books were old and priceless, though most students never bothered to look at them.

"Who'd bother stealing that stuff?" asked Melissa. "Some of those books are so ratty, they have green mold on them."

"Green mold." Jamie heard the words and knew instantly that he'd found a great title for his story. Yes, he would call it "The Green Mold Monster."

"Kids never look in that display case," said David.

"Well, you all should." Mrs. Eliot spoke sharply. "Why do I bother to rotate the exhibits if you children don't show interest?"

"What was stolen, anyway?" asked Henry.

"One of of our most precious volumes," said Miss Apthorp, taking a hankie from her pocket and nervously patting her brow. "It was one of Alexander Cartwright's own diaries; it covers the years he spent in Europe. An antiquarian bookshop once offered me a considerable sum for it, but naturally I refused to sell it."

"You should've sold it while you had the chance," Henry said. "What'd it look like?"

"It's a very old volume, bound in leather," Miss Apthorp explained. "It couldn't possibly have been mistaken for a library book. If anyone has a clue as to its whereabouts, please let me know."

"You'd better inform all the teachers of the theft," Mrs. Eliot suggested. "It may have been innocently misplaced."

"I hope so." Miss Apthorp sighed as she left the room.

Usually Jamie would have been more interested in such an incident. Solving perplexing puzzles was one of his fascinations. But at the moment he was too involved in his story. He hurriedly wrote down his third paragraph, then raised his hand. "Mrs. Eliot, is it all right if I pace? Sometimes when writers are plotting, they need to pace."

Mrs. Eliot suppressed a smile. "Of course, Jamie—pace if you like, as long as you don't disturb anyone."

Amy stared at her absolutely blank paper, then stared at her brother who paced back and forth by the window. What a grandstander he was!

As Jamie constructed his sentence in his mind, he glanced out the window thoughtfully. Just then a man hurried from the entrance of Hillcrest. He seemed to resemble Dr. Manheim. He was wearing a floppy black hat, a cape, and white gloves . . . and he was carrying a large leather volume under one arm. Jamie watched curiously as the old man glanced around to make certain no one was observing him.

Suddenly the clouds that had darkened the sky that morning finally separated, and the sun broke through. The moment the man saw the sun radiate in his direction, he cringed, as if struck by lightning. Then he quickly removed a pair of dark glasses from his pocket and put them on. He folded the floppy black hat down over his face for protection, then draped himself inside his black cape. With the leather volume clutched tightly against him, he ran across the school grounds.

Jamie blinked. The figure draped in black was racing like the wind! He ran so quickly, he was out of sight within seconds. Jamie blinked again. That couldn't have been Dr. Manheim. The old man could never have run as fast as that.

But if it wasn't the doctor, who was it? he wondered. And was that Alexander Cartwright's diary under his arm? If it was, then why had he stolen it?

It had all happened too quickly for Jamie to react. The mysterious man was gone and perhaps the diary had disappeared with him.

Chapter Five

AFTER SCHOOL THE TWINS WENT FOR THEIR WEEKLY RIDING lesson at Briarcliff Stables. They walked in silence, each reluctant to reveal his thoughts to the other.

Jamie was pondering the puzzling incident he had observed from the school window. Could there possibly be *two* men living in Monroe who wore white gloves, a floppy hat, and a cape? he wondered. Highly unlikely. In fact, the law of averages probably made it impossible! Yet logic told him he couldn't have seen the doctor running like the wind—and Jamie was devoted to logic.

Amy was still sulking. Her brother had ridiculed her theory that Dr. Manheim was a vampire, yet instinct told her it was accurate.

So they continued their walk in silence.

As they approached Briarcliff Stables Amy sniffed the pungent aroma of horses, eagerly anticipating her weekly ride on Bluebell. Amy had been riding Bluebell for years and loved the horse better than any other at Briarcliff. She checked her schoolbag to make certain she hadn't forgotten the sugar lumps and carrots.

Usually Amy spent several minutes talking to Bluebell and feeding her snacks before they went for their ride. Once when Bluebell slipped a shoe, Amy had asked to keep it. She had hung it over her bed as a good-luck charm. And ever since, Amy had also considered the horse her personal good-luck charm. Whenever she had problems, a brisk ride on Bluebell made Amy's worries fly away. She and the mare would race through the fields like the wind. Yes, Bluebell was a dear, sensitive horse who always seemed to know when Amy needed a good run.

At the entrance to Briarcliff, Amy sensed that things were not normal inside the stables. She knew her premonition was accurate when she saw Fred Weatherby approaching. Mr. Weatherby, the owner of the stables, had two horses by the reins. One was Pippin, the horse Jamie always rode—but the other one was not Bluebell.

"Hi, kids," Mr. Weatherby said. "I've got your horses all saddled up. Saucy here has already had a few runs today, but she'll still keep up a fast gait for you, Amy. She has a nice hack, so I think you'll like riding her."

Jamie took the gelding Pippin by the bridle reins and stroked his head. "Hi, fella, how've you been?" Pippin nuzzled Jamie's neck.

"You've made a mistake, Mr. Weatherby," said Amy. "I always ride Bluebell, don't you remember?"

35

"I know Bluebell's your favorite, but Saucy will give you a good ride, too. I never assign her to beginning-level students. Just creep up on her reins until she accepts the bit. Sometimes she lugs on the bit, but you'll figure out her stride soon enough."

Amy grew uneasy. "Something's happened to Bluebell, hasn't it, Mr. Weatherby?"

"Let's just say she's not feeling well today." The stable owner sounded evasive.

"I want to see her," Amy said. "Tell me what's wrong."

"It's probably nothing serious, Amy. Next week she'll be right as rain."

Amy was now certain something awful had happened to Bluebell. She declined the horse Mr. Weatherby offered her. Instead, she hurried toward the main stable where she stopped at Bluebell's stall. The mare was lying down on a bed of clean hay banked up against the side of the stall. Rick, the stable boy, was rubbing her down with a towel.

Amy gasped as she noticed the stream of blood spilling down Bluebell's neck! "What happened, Rick?"

"I don't know; she's been like this all day. I'm going to the tack room to get her a blanket."

As Rick opened the stall door Amy rushed inside. Usually Bluebell would whinny a greeting whenever she saw Amy, but the mare seemed too weak to notice her. As Amy began to stroke her, Bluebell broke into a cold sweat. Amy quickly dried her down with the sweat scraper, then patted her with the damp towel.

Mr. Weatherby passed by and leaned over the stall

door. "You shouldn't be in there, Amy," he cautioned. "I can't have students messing around with sick horses."

"*Why* is she sick? What's wrong with her?"

"It's probably just a nasty cut, but I can't figure how she got it. She was fine last night when Rick bedded her down, then this morning she had that mean gash on her throat. What worries me is, the darn thing won't stop bleeding."

As Jamie galloped by on Pippin, he slowed the horse to a trot. "Aren't you going for your ride?" he asked. He dismounted and glanced into Bluebell's stall. "Say, what's wrong with her? She looks awful."

Amy pressed the towel against the bloody slash on Bluebell's throat. "Has she been bleeding like this all day, Mr. Weatherby?"

"I'm afraid so."

"No wonder she's so weak. Can't you do something to stop the bleeding?"

"The vet is on his way, don't worry. You kids go for your ride now."

"No." Amy was firm. "I'm staying here with Bluebell."

Jamie took a closer look at the mare's wound. "Looks like she's been bitten by some animal, but that's impossible. What animal around here would bite a horse?"

Mr. Weatherby nodded. "That's exactly what I told the old man earlier today."

"What old man?" asked Amy.

"Oh, a peculiar old guy, with a big white mustache and black cape," explained Mr. Weatherby. "He said he'd come to inquire about lessons, but an old guy like that couldn't have been interested in riding. He'd probably break all his bones trying to mount one of my horses. He looked half-blind too. He wore such thick dark glasses, he could hardly see where he was going."

The twins stared at each other: Mr. Weatherby seemed to be describing *Dr. Manheim.*

"You say he wanted riding lessons?" asked Jamie.

"So he told me. But he insisted on seeing all my horses first. Between us, I think the old guy was a little off. Anyway, I figured I'd humor him, so I gave him a tour of the stables. When we got to Bluebell, this old guy seemed very upset about her injury. That's when he suggested it was an animal bite."

"Did he say what kind of animal?" Amy asked nervously.

Mr. Weatherby shrugged. "Not an animal exactly. He figured it was a bat's bite. The old guy told me he was a doctor and a zoologist, so he knew about such things. Well, I told him I've lived in Monroe all my life and I've never heard of vampire bats in the area! Sure, I know those things bite horses and livestock, but we have no bat caves around here."

Jamie took a closer look at Bluebell's wound. It was a razorlike slash; a piece of flesh was missing, and blood flowed from the wound in a constant trickle. "If Bluebell got this cut last night, the blood should've clotted by now."

Mr. Weatherby agreed. "That's why the old guy thought it was the bite of a vampire bat. He said bats have an anticoagulant substance in their saliva which makes a wound bleed for a long time."

38

"What else did the old man tell you?" asked Amy.

"Lots of stuff that didn't make sense."

"*Please* try to remember," she said. "It may be important."

Mr. Weatherby scratched his head. "Oh yeah, he told me something real strange. He said a few nights before a full moon is a bad time for vampire bats. That's when they go out foraging. I figured the guy was talking cuckoo, but he did scare me. Anyway I'm having the vet come by today. All my horses are getting tetanus shots. I don't think there are any bats on the prowl, but it doesn't hurt to be on the safe side."

"I think that's a good idea," Jamie said.

"You do?" Mr. Weatherby said. "Listen, do you kids happen to know this old guy?"

"We might," Amy answered. She stared down at Bluebell, who seemed to be growing weaker by the minute. "If it's who I think it is," she added, "you'd better pay attention to him."

Mr. Weatherby looked concerned. "No kidding? You really think there could be vampire bats in the area?"

"It sounds unlikely," said Jamie, "but I guess anything is possible."

Amy didn't have the heart to ride any other horse but Bluebell. While Jamie had his lesson, she sat in the mare's stall stroking her head and speaking to her softly. She hoped to get her to take a nibble of sugar or carrots, but the horse showed no interest in food.

Amy was so upset, she nearly cried. Horrid visions of vampire bats kept flashing through her mind, and she was more convinced than ever that Dr. Manheim was somehow responsible.

Amy was reluctant to leave Bluebell's stall, but Mr. Weatherby assured her the vet would be by shortly. "He'll fix her up in no time, don't worry. Next week she'll be galloping through the meadows again."

The twins began their walk home in silence—a silence that Jamie broke. "I've been thinking this deal over, Amy. Maybe you're not as nuts as I thought. Something weird happened to that horse, and Dr. Manheim knows something about it. He also stole Cartwright's manuscript from Hillcrest today. I saw him running from the building with it. At first I wasn't certain it was Manheim but now I'm sure."

Amy didn't seem surprised. "What are we going to do, Jamie?"

"Look for a logical explanation."

"But we already have the explanation. Dr. Manheim is a *vampire*."

"That's totally *illogical*—and ridiculous," Jamie argued. "But I agree with you that Dr. Manheim is up to something. We've got to find out what it is."

"How?"

"Maybe it wouldn't hurt to have another talk with Jebediah. If he knows something, now's the time for him to tell us!"

Chapter Six

THE MOON SHONE THROUGH AMY'S BEDROOM WINDOW. SHE and her brother had seated themselves on the floor, and Amy had placed one of Jebediah Tredwell's silver candlesticks on the rug. She now lit it.

"Do you think we should hold hands?" she asked.

"Quit the hocus-pocus stuff," said Jamie. "Can you get Jeb to materialize or not?"

"How should I know? He's not our servant, you know, Jamie. He's a free spirit!"

"Quit the puns, just concentrate." Jamie felt self-conscious, even awkward. Making contact with a ghost went against all his theories of a logical, orderly universe, and he wanted this business to be over as soon as possible. He was still miffed that Amy (who didn't have a brain in her head) could actually *see* their ancestor, while he (with his superior intelligence) couldn't. In Jamie's mind that fact defied all laws of justice and common sense.

Amy closed her eyes and concentrated. "Jebediah," she said softly, "are you here? We need to speak with you."

"Don't be so formal," said Jamie. "Call him Jeb or J.T. After all, he's family."

"Are you here, Jeb? If you are, please show yourself. It's awfully important."

Amy opened her eyes and glanced toward the darkened corner of the room, suddenly conscious of an intense energy field. Tiny particles of light emerged from the dark and quickly formed themselves into the figure of Lieutenant Colonel Jebediah Tredwell of the Continental army. The moonlight bounded off his gold epaulets, shiny black boots, and gleaming sword.

"Why have you called me forward thus, Cousin?" he asked.

"We need information, Jeb. You must tell us more about Dr. Manheim."

The spirit seemed obviously distressed. " 'Tis a wretched business, that. I perceive my position within it to be wretched as well. If only I might inform you candidly of my discontents—without disguise or palliation—I should be heartily glad of it. But you maintain an erroneous idea of my powers within your realm."

"You *have* to answer some questions for us," she said.

Jamie, unaware that Jebediah had appeared in the room, was growing impatient. "Forget it, he's not coming. Let's see if there's any dessert left."

42

"Don't leave now, stupid," Amy shouted. "Jeb is here in the room with us!"

Jamie glanced around. As usual he saw nothing.

He also heard nothing of Jebediah's robust laughter which now suddenly filled the room. "Your brother's mind must be insensible indeed, to be totally unaware of such an impressive figure as myself!"

Amy giggled.

"Did Jeb say something?" asked Jamie.

She nodded.

"Well, what did he say?"

"He thinks you're stupid too," she replied.

Jamie grew angry. "Thanks a lot, J.T.!"

Jebediah's laughter ceased. "Nay, Cousin, do not put words into my mouth. This is not a subject for jest. I have taken on the obligation of guiding you *both*, and it is a privilege to do so. If I am not deceived in the knowledge of myself, I may serve to enlighten some areas of your distress. But I should do injustice to my own feelings not to acknowledge the limits of my powers. Would that I could do more, I should be heartily glad of it."

"Jeb says he can't tell us much," Amy explained.

"He *has* to," Jamie said. "If Dr. Manheim is involved in something evil and we're involved, too, we've got to know what it is."

Jebediah's spirit moved across the room, his hands tucked inside his waistcoat. Then he glanced out the window toward the full moon. Its shimmering glow cast an iridescent light through his filmy presence. "Little did I imagine when I left the theater of life that I would ever

43

hear the name of Manheim again. Two centuries have passed and still the evil of his household remains. It darkened the door of Alexander Cartwright's ancestors more than once. Would that I could eradicate the havoc such creatures as he have unleashed."

"Why do you call Dr. Manheim a *creature*?" Amy asked. "Is it because he isn't human?"

"There can be no virtue in his practices," Jeb explained, "yet the darker aspects of mankind are human nonetheless. But if you were to ask me be he mortal, I would say I had cause for doubt. What I have seen is perhaps best left unseen and unspoken."

Jamie glanced around the room, wondering where Jeb's spirit might be. "Look, J.T., we need some concrete answers. What's the connection between Alexander Cartwright and Dr. Manheim? The old man stole Cartwright's diary today and we don't know why. If you've got any clues, spit them out!"

Jamie's revelation seemed both to surprise and to distress Jebediah. "Manheim has absconded with the diary? By all that is damnable, the man is more than a coward would choose to look upon! A pox on him!" The spirit began pacing the room angrily. "If I could but tell the truth in this matter, my spirit could be at ease once again. But my truth may not be the *whole* truth. Odzooks! I find my choices limited. Shall I cast an affront upon my fellow man? Will doing so entwine you further in his treachery? Zounds! I am confused."

"Did Jeb answer me?" asked Jamie.

"Sort of," Amy explained. "I think he's afraid we'll be in danger if he tells us anything."

"If he doesn't tell us, I'll find the answer myself," Jamie declared.

"That's true, Jeb. Jamie *will*, you know. He's awfully clever at figuring things out."

Jebediah nodded in agreement. "Then perhaps my secrecy is to no purpose." Once again the spirit stared out the window. Then he turned and began his explanation. "Very well, I shall propose my utmost and spare nothing. To this end, I must elaborate on one of my many European travels. As a young man, I once toured the countryside outside Leipzig with horse and coach. After passing over many intolerable roads, I required rest for my horses, and came upon a rather secluded hostelry where I met the proprietor, Heinrich Manheim."

"An ancestor of the doctor's?" asked Amy.

"Indeed so. I found him to be a genial, affable host. In return for his many courtesies I took it upon myself to invite him to my home, should he ever visit the Colonies. At a much later date, Heinrich Manheim accepted that invitation. At that time I observed him to be a man of frail stature and pale features, with a strange propensity for nocturnal wanderings. Through my instigation he soon became a friend of Enoch Cartwright, a man of much prominence in Monroe."

"And he was an ancestor of Alexander Cartwright?" asked Amy.

Jebediah nodded. "This much is unadulterated fact. What occurred thereafter must give one's reason pause.

The two men soon became inseparable, yet it seemed to be a friendship which had grave consequences for the parties involved. Hitherto Enoch Cartwright had been a robust, athletic sportsman, but shortly after Manheim's arrival Cartwright's health deteriorated drastically. He took to his room, secluding himself from his family and the world. From that point on, his face never again saw the light of day. He transacted all business at night. Disturbing tales began to circulate—tales regarding his strange nocturnal habits. Townsfolk said he often frequented the graveyard. Once when I had occasion to visit him at night, I came upon a grotesque visage. I was shocked to find the poor wretch had been afflicted by some strange malady which had caused his skin to become discolored and his teeth reddened. Moreover, he had taken to wearing gloves which he refused to remove. I was even more distressed to realize these were the very same characteristics I had begun to observe in Heinrich Manheim. Curious, to be sure."

Amy, disturbed by what Jebediah had said, suddenly felt faint. She swayed back and forth, then her head flopped to one side.

"What has made you to swoon, child?" asked the spirit. "Is it I who have caused you this distress?" He approached Amy and began to stroke her forehead. "One should never go without a bottle to smell or a feather to burn under the nose."

"What's wrong?" asked Jamie. "Are you okay, Amy? Is J.T. still here? What's he been telling you?"

As Amy took a deep breath she sensed the spirit's presence gradually recede.

"I have overstepped my bounds and revealed too much. Take care, child," he said. "There is danger here; mistake it not."

"No, don't go yet," she said. "Something weird happened at Briarcliff Stables last night. Bluebell, my favorite horse, was bitten by some animal. Do you think it could be—"

"The vile wretch!" Jebediah shouted. "Is there not sufficient field for his roguery and villainy upon the continent? Must he taint our shores with it? History indeed repeats itself, then. I must caution you, Cousin, similar attacks of viciousness occurred in my day as well. My own steed, Lightning, who rode onto the field of battle with me, was the victim of such an outrage!" Jebediah's figure suddenly began to fade. "Alas, my time within this realm is short. But list now: Not a word I have uttered has been a departure from truth. This much more I may say. I believe daylight to be Dr. Manheim's enemy, and therefore it is your friend. Should you have any further contact with this man, be certain it be before nightfall. Hear me well, Cousin, for I fear your life may depend upon it."

With those words Jebediah's spirit disappeared into the dark, and the candle blew out.

"It's just like I said," Amy declared. "Old Dr. Manheim is a *vampire*."

The twins were seated at the kitchen table. Jamie was

finishing off his midnight snack of peanut butter on a bagel, a bag of potato chips, and milk.

"It's just like *I* said," he argued, "you're jumping to conclusions."

"How can you eat all that junk before bed, Jamie? Aren't you afraid of having nightmares?"

Jamie gobbled down the last chip, then licked his finger to gather up the salt at the bottom of the bag. "Nightmares are the product of an overactive imagination, Amy—something *you* seem to be suffering from."

"I only repeated everything Jebediah told me," she said defensively.

"And I listened to every word you repeated. But not once did I hear you mention the word *vampire*."

"That's true," Amy said, "but maybe vampires weren't called that in Jebediah's day."

"Baloney. Vampire legends have existed for hundreds of years. But that's all they are, Amy, *legends*. And only superstitious people believe them. We're living in the twentieth century, not the Dark Ages."

Amy sighed. "I give up. You still won't believe *anything* Jeb told us?"

"Sure I do. There's definitely some connection between the Manheims and the Cartwrights. Mabye it *is* some family secret—but I'll bet it has something to do with *money*, not vampires. Miss Apthorp said that diary was valuable, remember? I'll bet that's the reason Manheim stole it. Maybe he needs cash to finance his research. Don't worry, we'll figure this whole thing out. After school tomorrow let's go over to the old Brewster place to pay Dr. Manheim a visit."

"I'm not sure that's a good idea, Jamie. It might not be safe."

"Relax," said Jamie, gulping down his milk. "Dr. Manheim may be a thief, but he's definitely not Dracula. Like I told you, that stuff is just in storybooks."

Chapter Seven

"How's the Green Mold Monster doing?" asked Mr. Ferguson at breakfast.

"It's coming along okay, Dad," said Jamie, "but writing a truly scary story isn't easy."

"Have you found an idea for your story yet, Amy?" her mother asked.

Amy, never much good at writing, felt the real events of the past two days were scarier than anything she could have imagined. "I haven't thought of a thing, Mom."

"Well, I'm sure you will. I think this competition is just right for Halloween. I've always loved being frightened on Halloween. Telling scary stories outdoors is a marvelous idea."

Jamie nodded. "It sure beats getting hit on the head with a sack of flour!"

"If you stop by the university after school," said Mr.

Ferguson, "you both could write in the library. Being surrounded by classic works of literature might be the inspiration Amy needs."

"No, thanks, Dad," said Jamie. "We already have our afternoon planned. We thought we'd go by the Brewster place and see how Dr. Manheim is getting along. I had a real interesting conversation with him the other night, and I thought he might like to come to dinner again."

"Certainly invite him," said Mr. Ferguson. "As long as your mom isn't serving *garlic* again."

"Don't remind me," said Mrs. Ferguson. "I'll never live down that dinner. The poor man practically starved!"

Mr. Ferguson buttered his toast. "I've a great idea for you, Amy. Why not write a nice gory vampire story? Vampires have an aversion to garlic, too, you know. In some areas of Europe people still hang bunches outside their doors to keep the creatures away. They supposedly have an aversion to mirrors too."

"I didn't know that," she said, and remembered Dr. Manheim's reluctance to pass in front of the mirror in their living room.

"Why sure, those old myths don't die easily, you know. Why not write a story in which the European garlic industry skyrockets because of an increase in the vampire population? Something like that might change the entire economy of a Balkan country. It might even make them eligible for the Common Market. A story like that could be an interesting socioeconomic statement, don't you think?"

"Richard, let Amy think up her own story," his wife said. "I don't want her plagiarizing someone else's idea."

"Isn't plagiarism stealing someone's *written* words, Miriam? Anyway, I'm merely throwing out possible story concepts, that's all. If you don't like that one, Amy, how about writing the history of Vlad the Impaler, the real-life Dracula."

"C'mon, Dad," said Jamie, "there's no real-life Dracula."

"There certainly was, Son. Only his name wasn't Bela Lugosi, it was Vlad Dracul. He was a prince of Transylvania who had a most unpleasant way of punishing those who displeased him. He liked to impale them alive on a stake so they'd die slowly with a maximum of suffering. In a two-year period, between 1459 and 1461, he impaled over twenty thousand prisoners. It's said he created an entire *forest* of impaled corpses near the Danube River. He not only impaled people, he also liked to roast the bodies and boil their heads in a kettle!"

Mrs. Ferguson put down her coffee cup; rattling it nervously. "Richard, don't talk about such dreadful things."

"It's *history*, Miriam; I didn't make it up. Vlad Dracul was a tyrannical monster. Besides, I thought you liked being frightened."

"Only by fiction, thank you."

"There are *real-life* monsters in the world, too, you know," he said. "One look at history will verify that. Imagine, just a few years before Columbus sailed to the Americas, Vlad Dracul was decimating the population of Europe with his butchery."

Amy felt a queasiness in her stomach. "Maybe I won't write anything for the contest, Dad. I guess I'm just not looking forward to Halloween this year."

"Then let's change the subject," said her mother. "If you two are planning to go by the Brewster place today, make sure you're home before nightfall. I don't want you wandering through those woods after sundown; you might get lost."

Amy shuddered, remembering Jebediah's warning. "Don't worry, Mom, we'll definitely be home before dark!"

The afternoon had suddenly turned cold and cloudy. Dry leaves crackled beneath the twins' feet as they moved through the woods on their way to the old Brewster place.

"Why do you suppose Mr. Brewster built that old house so far away from town?" Amy asked. "And so close to the graveyard too."

"He was probably a crook," Jamie said. "I'll bet he used that house for smuggling or as a hideout. Suspicious people never want anyone snooping around. As for the graveyard, well, you know what they say—Dead men tell no tales."

"My point exactly," Amy said apprehensively.

"Will you relax? That story Dad told this morning sure gave you the creeps, didn't it? This is *Monroe*, not Transylvania, Amy. C'mon, we've got to get in that house and sneak a peek at the stolen diary. When Manheim answers the door, be *charming*, okay? Otherwise you'll give the whole show away."

How do you charm a vampire? Amy wondered. "I bet we won't find one mirror in that house," she said, tripping over a gnarled tree branch.

"Watch where you're going," Jamie shouted.

They had come to a clearing in the woods, and now slowly they approached the old Brewster house. It was just as dilapidated as they'd remembered. Weeds covered the lawn; and shingles hung from the roof, just as they had when the twins played there years ago. None of the broken windows had been repaired, either, but they were now covered with dark, heavy draperies. The place looked just as solemn, abandoned, and unloved as ever.

"I guess Dr. Manheim isn't much of a fixer-upper," Jamie said. "Maybe Mom could get our housekeeper, Mrs. Romanoff, to come over. She was right about this place: it needs a woman's touch."

"It needs a bulldozer!"

Jamie pressed on the door bell; it had rusted solid. Then he banged the old metal knocker; it, too, was rusty.

They waited several minutes, but no one answered. Just as Jamie was about to peek through one of the broken windows, he noticed the draperies move. Someone was watching them from inside. They heard stumbling noises, as if someone or something had fallen. Then there were footsteps moving hurriedly up the stairs.

Jamie banged the knocker again. Presently the door creaked on its rusty hinges and Dr. Manheim appeared from behind it. As usual he was wearing his white gloves, but he seemed to have put them on in haste. One glove only half covered his wrist. Amy gasped as she noticed the thick black hair covering the exposed portion of the doctor's hand. It looked like the hair of an animal, not a human!

"It is I who should be startled," said Dr. Manheim. "You children are my first visitors, which is indeed a pleasure. I keep such strange hours, I've little time to socialize." Adjusting his gloves, he swung the door wide open and ushered the twins inside.

The house looked like a dark, cluttered cave. The thick draperies shut out any light that might have entered. Books and papers were scattered over the dusty tables and dingy upholstered furniture. Several packing crates were piled underneath the staircase that led upstairs. In the living room a candelabrum rested on an upright piano, which was missing most of its keys. The candelabrum was the only source of light in the room, and its flickering flame caste eerie shadows across an overstuffed Victorian sofa and chairs.

Dr. Manheim noticed the look of surprise on the children's faces. "The electricity hasn't been turned on yet," he explained. "In a few days I hope to have the place put right. An old bachelor like myself is willing to put up with clutter. I find my work so absorbing, I hardly notice it."

Jamie glanced furtively around the room, hoping to catch a glimpse of the stolen diary. It was nowhere in sight. "We haven't been in this house for ages," he said. "Me and Amy used to sneak in the windows and play hide-

and-seek upstairs. Naturally, we were much younger. There was a big old closet up there I loved to hide inside. You don't mind if I go up and look at it, do you?"

"I most certainly do," the doctor said sternly. "The upstairs rooms are in even worse disrepair. Two of the steps are broken as well. As a matter of fact, I've been forced to sleep in the dining room. I can't use the bedrooms until a carpenter repairs the steps."

Jamie's quick observations told him that wasn't altogether true. From the foot of the stairs he observed one of the bedroom doors. Shiny new locks and bolts had been installed. Remembering the sound of footsteps running up the stairs, he knew someone must be up there.

Dr. Manheim removed the clutter from the sofa and offered the children a seat. "To what do I owe the honor of your visit?"

"We wanted to invite you to dinner again," Jamie said. "I'm really interested in zoology, and I thought we might talk some more."

"Indeed? It's clear you have a quick mind, Jamie, so I'm sure many fields interest you. And what about you, Amy?" the doctor asked. "Are you interested in my occupation as well?"

Amy had been staring at Dr. Manheim. He seemed more robust and youthful than she had remembered, and there was even a touch of pink in his cheeks. What, she now wondered, had caused the sudden change? Bluebell's blood perhaps?

"No," she said aloud, in answer to the doctor's question. "I mean—well, I do like animals—especially horses. There are some lovely horses at Briarcliff Stables. Have you been there?"

The doctor's response was somewhat evasive. "Riding is a hobby for those with leisure time, of which I have little. But where are my manners? Perhaps you children would like some tea?"

The twins stared at each other. Amy was wondering if it was safe to accept the old man's offer. What strange substance might he slip into the teapot along with the leaves? "Just some water," she said. (You could always tell when something had been added to water, she reasoned.)

Jamie hoped that while the doctor was in the kitchen, he could poke around the living room in search of the diary. But Dr. Manheim left the kitchen door open, which made that impossible.

The twins sat stiffly on the sofa, where the doctor could observe them from the doorway. "Something sneaky is going on," Jamie mumbled. "The old guy has put locks on the bedroom door. He's definitely hiding something up there."

"And he lied about being at the stable," Amy muttered.

"Right, but let's not arouse his suspicions. Can you get some psychic message about where that diary is hidden?"

"I'll try," she whispered.

The doctor returned with the water and handed a glass to Amy. She stared at his white gloves, remembering the horrid hairy sight they kept hidden. Taking the glass, Amy gazed into the clear liquid. Its fluid transparency seemed like a crystal, through which one could observe many sights normally unseen to the human eye. There, within the liquid, an image of the stolen manuscript came into focus. It was locked inside the old oak desk in the corner of the room!

Concentrating her psychic energy, Amy could see that the diary was opened to a particular page, which she began reading:

Leipzig, March 17, 1930. So far, I've made lots of friends here at the university. There's one strange young medical student, Gustav Manheim, who seems to be involved in his own personal experiments. He never socializes and refuses to let any of us into his room. When I spoke to him the other day, I told him I thought we had ancestors who knew one another long ago. Gustav acted very strangely when I told him that. He said I must be mistaken. He's certainly a peculiar man—brilliant, but peculiar. I wonder what he keeps locked up in his room. Dangerous chemicals, probably. He must have already burned himself, badly, because he wears gloves all the time. . . .

As the image of the diary began to fade, Amy received another vision. There was something else hidden inside the desk. Another manuscript—much older. Another *diary*. And this one was stolen as well. It had recently been taken from the library of Monroe's Historical Society. The pages were yellow and fragile. The ink was slightly faded, but a picture of the script came into focus:

Leipzig, May 19, 1794. My search is finally at an end. For more than a decade I have pursued the monster who has made me like unto himself. Each dawn I curse the day I first came into contact with Heinrich Manheim, but now I shall finally take vengeance for his evildoing. At last I know the whereabouts of the crypt which has eluded me for so long. I dare not seek it out in daylight, lest the sun reveal me for the vile wretch I now am. Alas, I curse the heavens for this cruel irony. Only at night am I allowed to show myself. And yet night is Manheim's slave and conspirator. Somehow, I must trap him at dawn, when he is at my mercy. But I grow weak and the desire for fresh blood ofttimes is uncontrollable. I pray my quest is successful, lest this curse pass on through further generations of Cartwrights. . . .

Suddenly the pages become blurred and the vision was gone. Amy's body stiffened as she dropped the glass from her hand. Hearing it shatter to the ground, she found herself back in reality. "I'm sorry," Amy said, and began to pick up the pieces. A tiny sliver pricked her finger, and she began to bleed.

Dr. Manheim gasped when he saw the red fluid trickle down Amy's hand. He stared at it in fascination, then suddenly he turned his eyes away and removed a handkerchief from his pocket. "Have you cut yourself badly?"

"It's just a scratch."

Looking slightly faint, Dr. Manheim sat down. "You must take care," he said. "I have no medical supplies on hand. That's ironic, isn't it? A doctor with no medical supplies."

Jamie was growing uneasy. "We've got lots of Band-Aids at home." He glanced at his watch. "Can I tell my parents you'll come to dinner soon?"

"Yes, perhaps this weekend." Dr. Manheim noticed Jamie's watch. "What a handsome timepiece."

"It was my grandfather's," the boy exclaimed. "On our twelfth birthday I got this watch and Amy got our grandmother's gold locket. They've both been in the family for generations."

Dr. Manheim nodded. "Yours is a family of tradition—as is mine. A strange thing, tradition, don't you agree? At times it can be a tyrant, stealing one's free will. Because of tradition, things are often done not because we want to do them but because we must."

"I've never thought of it like that," Jamie said nervously. He was afraid Manheim now suspected they had come to snoop. They would surely arouse his suspicions further if they made too quick a getaway . . . but Jamie was anxious to speak with Amy, to learn if she had received any psychic clues about where the manuscript might be hidden. "Well," he said casually, "we'd better leave before it starts getting dark. It's hard to find your way through those woods after nightfall."

"Yes," the doctor said, ushering the twins to the door. "Many things are hidden by the cloak of darkness."

As they reached the entrance a strange screech came from somewhere upstairs. Then there was a plaintive moan, as if someone were crying for help. Glancing toward the stairs, Jamie thought he saw the padlock on the bedroom door begin to shake. Then there was a thumping sound, as if someone were pounding on the door, attempting to get out.

Dr. Manheim heard it too. "Old houses settling make such peculiar sounds, don't they? The wind through broken windows can seem quite eerie at times. Well, children, give your parents my best regards and tell them I shall see them both very soon."

Before either of the twins could say another word, Dr. Manheim had slammed the door in their faces. They could hear him bolt it from inside.

"Let's get out of here," said Amy. "I've something important to tell you."

Jamie noticed a large enamel box tucked away on the side of the porch. "Just a minute." He tiptoed over to examine it. A plug extended from the back, through an opening in the kitchen window. "Look at this, Amy; it's a deep freeze. Manheim must've lied about the electricity being off. Whatever is in here is frozen solid."

"What's inside?"

"Crates. They're all hammered shut. Wait. They've got some writing on them." Jamie tried to decipher the words. "I think it's in Latin."

"Are you sure it's not German?"

Jamie examined the words stamped in red on each

crate: *Desmodus rotundus, Diaemus youngi, Dyphylla ecaudata.*
"I'm pretty sure that's Latin, Amy."

"Gosh, it sounds like some evil incantation. It must be a *curse.*"

Jamie slammed down the lid of the freezer, then glanced anxiously toward the woods. The wind was beginning to rustle the trees, and dusk was falling fast. "Let's get out of here," he said. "Right now!"

When the twins arrived home, Jamie made a hasty call to Roger Evansby, a Latin instructor at Monroe University. The children knew most of the professors at the university personally, which came in handy whenever Jamie had a question. And Jamie often had questions on any number of subjects.

"Amy and I have a bet," he explained. "She says the words mean some kind of curse, and I say they don't. Could you help us out, Mr. Evansby?"

"I'll try, Jamie. Would you repeat them for me again?"

"Desmodus rotundus, Diaemus youngi, Dyphylla ecaudata."

As her brother repeated the words Amy got a creepy feeling. Could he be conjuring up demons without knowing it?

There was a pause on the other end of the telephone.

"Well, Mr. Evansby? Do you know what it means?"

"I think so. You might want to check this out with a zoologist, but as far as I know, those are the names of three types of vampire bats."

"Jamie Ferguson, you're the most stubborn, pigheaded person in the entire world!" Amy shouted.

62

The twins were seated in the kitchen having another midnight snack. Actually, Jamie was having the snack and Amy was having a minor fit! She couldn't believe that all the evidence they had piled up hadn't yet convinced her brother that Dr. Manheim was a vampire.

"We have to go to the police," she said. "Manheim should be arrested before something terrible happens."

Jamie filled a bowl with his third helping of Heavenly Hash ice cream, then poured on some chocolate syrup. "Sure, Amy, you do that," he said smugly. "But don't forget to tell them how you know where Alexander Cartwright's stolen diary is hidden . . . and how you know about Enoch Cartwright's diary, which was stolen from the Historical Society. *No one* knows about that yet. But you just tell them you had a psychic vision."

"No, Jamie, I couldn't. If I did, everyone would know about my powers, and I don't want anyone to know."

"Exactly. If you don't reveal your powers, we have no evidence of a robbery."

"But we can't just forget it. Dr. Manheim's ancestors turned Enoch Cartwright into a vampire too."

"Who says? Enoch Cartwright might've been *insane.* Anyway, both manuscripts are locked in Manheim's desk, and we can't get a search warrant without some reason."

"How about Manheim's hairy hands? Isn't that a reason?"

Jamie shrugged. "Dr. Manheim could be hairy as a gorilla. So what? Being hairy isn't breaking the law."

Amy was becoming frustrated. "Well, how about the vampire bats?"

"Since when is it a crime to keep frozen bats?"

"But *why* is he keeping them, Jamie? You don't suppose they were once *people*, do you? And who has he got locked upstairs?"

The barrage of questions left Jamie unfazed. Indeed he was becoming even more fascinated with the mystery. "It's certainly a puzzle, isn't it? You know your problem, Amy? You overdramatize everything. You think the entire world is weird just because you sometimes see one measly ghost."

"Don't let Jebediah hear you call him measly," she said.

Jamie rinsed his bowl in the sink. "Sometimes I wonder if you haven't made up this whole business with Jebediah."

"*What?*"

"Okay, so you actually do see him. You haven't enough imagination to make up a thing like that. But as for me, I like to deal in facts. So far the only real fact is that Dr. Manheim is a thief who seems to be hiding something in his house."

"Something or *someone*," Amy said. "Remember what he told us when we first met him? He said *two* had come with him to this country. Two *what*? I wonder. Two more vampires, probably." Once again Amy saw a vision of the weird woman wandering through the graveyard. "I know one of them is a woman," she added.

Jamie yawned. "I can't think clearly when I'm tired. Whatever's going on, we can't solve it tonight. I'm going to bed; it's after midnight." As he switched off the kitchen

64

light, he heard a strange howl from somewhere outside. He glanced out the window. "It's a full moon," he said. "Some dog must be howling at it."

Amy shivered. The unearthly moan sounded nothing like a dog howling!

Chapter Eight

AT BREAKFAST THE NEXT MORNING THE EGGS WERE RUNNY AND the bacon was burned.

"Sorry," Mrs. Ferguson said, "I didn't sleep too well. I heard dreadful noises all night."

Jamie poked the outer edges of his egg as his father pushed his own plate aside.

"I'll just have coffee," Mr. Ferguson said. Taking a sip, he frowned. "Miriam, it's black. You know I can't drink black coffee."

"You'll have to, there's no milk. Crowley's Dairy Farm didn't deliver this morning. I called earlier and they said their cows had taken ill. There'll be no milk deliveries for a while."

"Taken ill?" he asked. "With what?"

Mrs. Ferguson yawned. "Some virus, I guess. Mr. Crowley said they were bitten by something. I was too sleepy to get the details. I'll stop by the supermarket later and pick up some powdered milk."

Amy kicked her brother underneath the table. "Did you hear that? Mr. Crowley's cows were *bitten* by something. Isn't that terrible?"

Jamie was still trying to salvage the outer unburned edges of his bacon. "What?"

"Mr. Crowley's cows were *bitten*," she repeated. "In the *neck*, I'll bet." Amy grimaced, pointing to her teeth.

Mr. Ferguson stared at his daughter. "Are you all right this morning? Why are you making weird faces?"

"No reason, Dad. It's just that sometimes Jamie fails to see the nose on his own face and doesn't know a fact when he falls over it!"

"Is that so? Well, what fact have you fallen over that Jamie fails to recognize?"

To Amy's surprise, her brother blurted it out: "Amy thinks weird things are going on at the Brewster place. When we stopped by there yesterday, Dr. Manheim seemed to have something hidden upstairs. He also keeps frozen bats in a freezer."

To Amy's further surprise, her father merely smiled and said, "That sounds typical of Gustav Manheim. I think he may be the prototype for the term *mad scientist*."

"You don't think it strange that he keeps bats?" Amy asked.

"No, bats obviously have something to do with his research. The doctor's secretiveness isn't odd either. Science can be a cutthroat business: for the scientist this means vying for grants, publishing papers before someone beats you to the punch—not to mention coming up with new discoveries before someone else does. A cloak of mystery has always surrounded scientific projects, especially Gustav Manheim's projects. I wouldn't be surprised at anything he might have hidden in the Brewster place. He selected that old house so that no one would undermine his research."

Jamie stuck his tongue out at his sister. "See, I told you, stupid. You have to think *logically*."

"That still doesn't explain why—" Amy stopped herself abruptly. She was about to mention what she'd read in the stolen diary, but realized that would reveal her psychic power.

"Explain what?" her father asked.

"Nothing, Dad. I guess I just don't like Dr. Manheim."

"I see. By the way, your mother and I are going to his seminar tonight. We'll be home late, so don't pig out on TV while we're gone."

Mr. Ferguson gulped down what remained of his black coffee. "I hope Crowley's cows get better quickly. I despise black coffee."

Amy poked at her uneaten breakfast and brooded.

She felt Crowley's dairy cows would *never* recover—not while Dr. Manheim was living in Monroe.

Jamie was silent during the walk to school. Unusually silent. Amy knew that meant he was thinking. In fact, she could almost visualize the tiny computer chips registering information in his brain.

"I've got it," he said. "I've figured it all out logically

and it makes sense." They stopped by a bench near Miller's Pond, and Jamie elaborated. "Fact one: Dr. Manheim stole Alexander Cartwright's diary because it mentioned research Manheim was working on over fifty years ago when he was a medical student. Fact two: Manheim is *still* working on that same project, and he's still just as secretive about it. Maybe his ancestor, Heinrich, was working on exactly the same thing two hundred years earlier when Jeb knew him. So here comes the big question: What could it be? What secret has eluded science for hundreds of years? What's been harder to accomplish than putting a man on the moon? What experiment might make a person grow hair on strange parts of his body? What discovery could a family spend generations working on?"

"I give up," said Amy. "What?"

"A cure for baldness," Jamie said smugly. "Why didn't I think of it sooner. Dr. Manheim hasn't perfected it yet. So far he can only make hair grow on hands. When he figures out how to grow it on heads, the guy will be a billionaire!"

"That's ridiculous. Besides, it doesn't explain the frozen bats."

"Yes, it does," he argued, thrilled with his own deductions. "Bat droppings are used for a fertilizer that's called guano. What if the stuff can fertilize *hair follicles* too? I'll bet Manheim is involved in the most stupendous discovery of the century. No wonder he's keeping it secret."

"Where's your evidence?" Amy asked. "You're always blabbing to me about evidence and you have none—just

69

a goofy theory I don't believe. Dr. Manheim is evil, or else Jeb wouldn't have warned us about him."

"Jeb's only human—at least he used to be. He could've been mistaken; in fact, he said he might be. J.T. saw a guy with hairy hands and jumped to conclusions, just like you did. I know I'm right, Amy, and I'll prove it. Tonight, when everyone's at the seminar, we'll sneak back to the Brewster place!"

"I never should've let you talk me into this," Amy grumbled.

As they approached the darkened entrance to the woods, the sound of bullfrogs croaking in Miller's Pond filled the night air. Usually Amy loved the night sounds of nature, but now they seemed ominous and threatening. "Jebediah warned us never to mess with Dr. Manheim after dark."

"Relax," said Jamie. "Manheim is at the university by now, and so are Mom and Dad. By the time they return, we'll have solved the whole mystery."

"Why are you so determined to do that?"

"Once I prove I'm right, maybe I can talk Manheim into making me his assistant. If I were a little older, we could start a *company* together. Manheim's hair-restoring formula could make me a teenage tycoon! I could stop wondering about a career because I'd be a *millionaire*."

Amy was skeptical. "The whole thing still sounds wacky to me. I never heard of a family working on one project for over two hundred years."

"That's nothing in scientific terms," he said. "I'll bet the ancient Egyptians were working on a cure for baldness too. That's probably why they wore those funny braided wigs. In Jeb's day they wore those funny powdered ones. I'm sure everyone was probably bald as a billiard ball."

Jamie switched on his flashlight as they made their way down the path leading to the woods.

As Amy stumbled through the dense underbrush, she heard the screech of a night owl overhead. "Let's turn back," she said pleadingly.

Jamie flashed the light in his sister's face. "Know your problem, Amy? You lack *initiative*. All our lives I've been the one to figure out practical problems while you've either been daydreaming or seeing ghosts. It's time you shaped up. Do you want to go through life like a scared rabbit, always running from shadows?"

"No! It's just that . . ."

"What?"

"Never mind." Amy grabbed the flashlight from her brother. She pushed him aside, then began to lead the way through the woods. Maybe everything Jamie said was *true*, she told herself. After all, Jebediah had admitted he might be mistaken about Dr. Manheim. It could all be some horrible mistake, with a perfectly logical explanation.

"Thatta girl," said Jamie, patting his sister's shoulder. "You'll soon see I'm right about everything. Once we get into Manheim's laboratory, the mystery will be solved."

"Then what'll you do?" she asked. "*Blackmail* the old man into making you his assistant?"

"Don't be crude. I merely plan to impress him with my

intelligence, initiative, and deductive reasoning. Remember what Dad said—it's never too early to plan my future; so if I can become part of a billion-dollar project, why shouldn't I?"

As the twins approached the clearing the old Brewster place came into view. Its massive dark shape was silhouetted by the moonlight, and it seemed more ominous and deserted than ever.

"Switch off that flashlight," Jamie whispered, "just in case someone's around."

They slowly tiptoed toward the entrance. The house seemed silent as a tomb. The old ladder the twins had once used in their game of hide-and-seek was still propped against the side porch.

"Good, nothing has changed," Jamie observed, "so there'll be no problem getting in upstairs." He started climbing the ladder. "Be careful, these rungs are real shaky."

"You climb inside first," said Amy, "while I keep an eye on the front door."

As Jamie ascended the ladder the rotting boards creaked under his feet. Slowly he pushed open the bedroom window, then poked his head inside and flashed the light around. The room was empty, except for a rusty metal bed and an old dresser. How disappointing. No test tubes, no laboratory table, no strange potions bubbling in beakers—nothing. Jamie climbed inside, then shouted down to his sister: "C'mon up, the coast is clear."

Amy went up the ladder and in through the bedroom window.

"I don't get it," said Jamie. "There's no evidence of anything up here."

"What'd you expect? If Dr. Manheim's research is top secret, he probably has everything locked up."

"That's right. His lab must be in that locked bedroom off the staircase. C'mon, let's look."

The twins tiptoed across the room, opened the bedroom door, and glanced down the corridor. The house was eerily silent. Jamie flashed the light toward the padlocked door. "That's odd," he said as they approached it, "the key is still in the lock. I guess old Manheim is the typical absentminded professor." He quickly turned the key and undid the lock.

"Wait," Amy said haltingly, "maybe we shouldn't go in there. What if . . ."

"What if I'm right and you're wrong? Relax, I won't say I told you so. Anyway, I *know* I'm right. Behind this door is evidence of Dr. Manheim's hair-restoring formula."

Jamie pushed open the door dramatically, as if the gesture itself were saying "I told you so" to his sister's skepticism. Then he stepped to one side of the doorway. "You look first, then tell me what you see. Beakers, right? Test tubes, right? Picture charts of bald heads, am I right?"

Amy flashed the light around the room. "Nothing," she said.

Jamie grabbed the flashlight. "That's impossible; there has to be something."

An unpleasant musty odor filled the large master bed-room. For a moment a chilly breeze parted the dark draperies which hung across the window. There were stacks of packing crates piled on the floor, and several lumpy comforters had been thrown on top of the four-poster bed in the corner.

Jamie walked around the room, scratching his head. "The old guy must be cleverer than I thought. Let me figure this out." He sat on the edge of the bed to think. "His lab must be in the *basement*," he said. "But then why did Manheim lock up an empty room? It doesn't make sense." As Jamie leaned back he felt something hard and lumpy underneath his hand. "Hey, there's something in this bed," he shouted, jumping off the mattress. As he did, the comforter slipped to the ground.

Underneath lay a very large, very bald man. His hands were crossed over his chest, and his body was rigid. His glassy eyes stared up at the ceiling, and his mouth hung open.

And he wasn't breathing!

"It's a *dead* man!" Amy shouted.

"It can't be," Jamie said, and leaned over to take a better look. He flashed the light directly on the figure. The man's skin seemed white and bloodless. Jamie touched the cheek. It was ice-cold. He lifted an arm to take the pulse, but he couldn't find one.

Jamie had never seen a dead body before, but this one certainly seemed as dead as anyone could get. He quickly pulled away, dropping the man's arm. But the arm did not fall back on the bed. Instead, it remained in the air, rigid as a poker.

"How horrible," Amy gasped. "He looks like he's pointing at something."

"No, I think that's called rigor mortis," said Jamie. "Maybe that's why dead bodies are called stiffs. I wonder who he is and how long he's been here. You suppose Dr. Manheim knows there's a dead man in his bedroom?"

"Of course he knows; he probably killed him. You'd better check his neck for puncture marks."

Jamie, normally cool in a crisis, suddenly grew frightened. A dead man didn't fit in with his theory! True, he was a *bald* dead man, but that didn't ease Jamie's apprehension. "We'd better get out of here, Amy." He grabbed his sister's hand, and together they hurried toward the door.

As they neared the staircase the twins stood frozen in terror. Along the ledge of the banister were several bats hanging upside down.

Amy screamed and threw herself into her brother's arms, which made Jamie drop his flashlight. They heard it roll down the stairs and then fall between the broken floorboards. The house was now in total darkness.

"What'd you do that for?" Jamie shouted, groping his way along the wall. "Now we can't see a thing."

"Don't pinch at my neck like that," Amy yelled through the darkness.

"I'm not pinching you, stupid," Jamie shouted.

Amy clamped her hand over her neck. A warm lumpy

object had perched there. "A vampire bat is attacking me!" she screamed, smacking at it hysterically.

Suddenly the twins could hear the sound of dozens of wings fluttering above their heads. Within moments the entire corridor and staircase landing became filled with bats. The children cringed and huddled against the wall as bat wings smacked against their bodies and horrid screeching sounds pierced their ears.

Amy's dreadful vision had become a horrible reality. "We'll never get out of here alive!" she cried.

Jamie, fumbling through the darkness, managed to find the staircase. "Follow the sound of my voice," he shouted.

As Amy frantically groped her way toward the sound of her brother's voice, she felt another bat clamp itself on her head. She practically ripped out a handful of hair trying to remove it. Then she, too, finally found the staircase, and they both hurried down the steps.

Near the foot of the stairs Jamie tripped and fell through a broken floorboard. His ankle was wedged between the rotting planks. He pulled it loose, then limped toward the front door and hurled it open. The children escaped into the darkness.

Neither one of them had ever run so fast. Jamie's ankle throbbed with pain, but he ran anyway. Amy's head pounded as she heard the screech of the bats fluttering behind them, but still she ran. Escape was uppermost in their minds—escape and putting as much distance between themselves and the dreadful sights they had witnessed within the Brewster house.

They had been running for several minutes when Jamie

stopped to catch his breath. It was then that he realized they had made a dreadful mistake. They had not been running toward the woods. Instead, they now found themselves at the entrance of the old graveyard.

The old Miller Cemetery had not been used for years. It was technically on the outskirts of the township, so the property had been abandoned. Most of the headstones had sunk into the ground and were covered with moss. Townspeople often said, "Only worms visit the old graveyard."

"We can't stop here," Amy said, quite breathless.

"We'll have to," Jamie said, still panting. His ankle was beginning to swell, and he couldn't continue running. Hobbling toward a gravestone, he propped himself up against it. "At least those bats have stopped chasing us." He sighed. "I need to rest awhile before we turn back."

Amy leaned against a gravestone too. "You and your brilliant ideas," she grumbled. "Only an *idiot* would visit a vampire's house at night. Now we're stuck in the graveyard. With our luck, it'll probably rain any minute."

As Amy spoke, they both heard the sound of thunder in the distance.

Jamie groaned. "Why'd you open your big mouth? What's next? I wonder." A bolt of lightning flashed through the sky. "Sorry I asked. Okay, let's get moving."

"Wait," Amy said. She had heard a strange sound close by. "What's that noise?"

Jamie listened too. It wasn't the screech of bats or the fluttering of wings. It was the crunch of footsteps tread-

77

ing over dried leaves. "Someone must've followed us," he whispered.

"Dr. Manheim?"

"I don't know; let's duck behind this gravestone and get out of sight."

As they hid behind the gravestone, thunder crackled ominously overhead and storm clouds partially obliterated the moon's light. Everything became unnaturally silent for a moment. The children realized this was merely the proverbial calm before a storm. Presently, the stillness was broken by the sound of approaching footsteps. Then there was a strangely plaintive cry, as if someone were singing a very sad song. As the cry grew louder, the twins saw a woman approaching. She was draped in a long white robe and wandered among the tombstones. Long black hair cascaded down her back. In her outstretched hands she carried a small black box. She stared straight ahead, totally unaware of her surroundings, and moved through the graveyard as if hypnotized. Each time she approached a gravestone she would emit another strange musical sound, then continue on.

"That's the woman in my vision," Amy whispered.

"I wonder who she is." Jamie said. "She looks like the bride of Dracula!"

"*You* said it, *I* didn't."

"Well, at least she's not after *us*. She doesn't seem to know we're here. I wonder what she's looking for."

"*Blood,* I'll bet," Amy said somberly.

"She's not getting mine," Jamie said, and crawled out from behind the gravestone.

As the woman glided through the cemetery, the twins began running in the other direction. They heard another clap of thunder in the distance, then rain began to fall. Soon the ground had turned to sloppy mud. Amy clutched her brother's arm as they ran. Then she tripped over a broken tree branch lying in their path, and they both tumbled into a deep hole. Jamie had fallen in first, and Amy landed on top of him.

"What happened?" Jamie shouted, trying to claw his way back up. Each time he clamped his hands onto the earthen wall, more damp dirt fell into the hole.

"This is an open grave," Amy grasped. "We've fallen into a *grave*."

"It must be a *well*," Jamie said. "No one has been buried in this place for years, so who'd dig a new grave?"

It rained heavily. Water filled the hole and gradually soaked through the children's sneakers.

"It *isn't* a new grave," said Amy ominously, "it's an old one. That must mean somebody was dug up recently!"

"Quit being the voice of doom," Jamie snapped. He clamped his feet along the sides of the hole, managing to boost himself up. Amy did the same. As they were about to climb out of the ditch, they saw something that made them change their mind.

The dead body that they had left in Dr. Manheim's bedroom was walking through the graveyard!

The man's legs were rigid, and his eyes had the look of death, but he was walking—toward *them*.

They ducked back into the hole and covered their faces. They could hear the dead man's footsteps on the wet ground. *Stomp, stomp, stomp*, the foosteps approached the grave. Then *stomp, stomp stomp*, they walked past it. The cemetery was silent once again. The thunder and lightning stopped.

For a moment the twins were afraid to remove their hands from their faces, uncertain what the next horrible sight might be. Gradually Jamie separated his fingers and glanced up. The clouds had parted again, and the moon was visible.

Jamie quickly crawled out of the ditch and Amy followed. They raced through the cemetery, past the Brewster house, and into the woods. They didn't stop running until they had reached Miller's Pond.

Occasionally they were tempted to look back, but they dared not.

If someone or something was following them, they did not want to know about it!

Chapter Nine

THE NEXT MORNING, THE TWINS SPRAYED SNEEZY GERMS ACROSS the breakfast table.

"Whatever possessed you two to go for a nature walk last night?" their father asked.

Amy blew her nose. "It was Jamie's idea. He was trying to prove one of his half-baked theories—which turned out to be all wet!"

Mrs. Ferguson placed steaming cups of tea with honey in front of the children. "No school for you guys today. Maybe I should have Dr. Cochran look at that ankle, Jamie."

"It's okay, I just fell in a hole."

"Well, you're both staying home," his mother repeated. "You can finish your English reports. Mrs. Romanoff will make you soup for lunch. I've asked her to work until this evening."

The twins had always loved their housekeeper's soup. Mrs. Romanoff added exotic herbs from the old country which made it taste unlike anything their mother ever prepared.

"Right, lots of rest and liquids and you kids'll be better by Halloween on Friday," said Mr. Ferguson. "Mom and I will call you tonight to see how you're doing."

"Where you going?" asked Amy.

"To visit eccentric Aunt Edith," her mother explained. "We're taking her into the city for her yearly shopping spree."

Since the twins were little, they had heard their great-aunt referred to as eccentric-Aunt-Edith, and for years they had assumed that was her first name! Edith Fortescue was a recluse who only left her house once a year for a shopping marathon in the city. She would stock up on everything from toothbrushes to a color TV, then retreat back into seclusion for another year.

"I'm afraid Aunt Edith has a long list this year," said Mr. Ferguson, "so it'll be a late night. I hope the car holds out. Last year we got a flat tire on the highway. With so much contraband in the trunk, I felt like a smuggler."

"Mrs. Romanoff is leaving at eight o'clock," said Mrs. Ferguson. "I'd like you children in bed early. No more wandering around in the woods, okay?"

Jamie sprayed another shower of sneezes across the room. "Don't worry, Mom, we're not going *anywhere*!"

By noon the comforting aroma of Helena Romanoff's chicken soup with dumplings (made from a secret Romanian recipe) filled the Ferguson kitchen. To Amy, it signified all the best aspects of home. Following her recent ordeal, she now felt safe, warm, and protected again.

Jamie, on the other hand, felt totally frustrated. As he analyzed the incidents of the night before, logic and reason seemed to be fighting a losing battle with the supernatural—something he found difficult to accept.

"Okay, so you don't believe *me*," Amy said, "but you should believe your own eyes. That old man we saw last night must've been a zombie—and that woman was definitely a *vampire*!"

Mrs. Romanoff, overhearing their conversation, nearly dropped the soup bowls to the ground. "It isn't funny to make such jokes," she said, her face turning pale.

"I wasn't joking," Amy said.

Mrs. Romanoff's hands began to shake. She placed the dishes on the table and stroked her forehead with her apron. Then she sat down, feeling slightly faint.

Jamie could see his sister's casual reference to vampires had obviously disturbed the old woman. "Amy didn't mean that," he said, hoping to reassure her. "We're writing scary stories for English class, that's all."

Mrs. Romanoff breathed a sigh of relief. "When I come to this country, I pray I will never hear the word *vampire* again. In my little village in Romania many suffered the curse of the undead."

"You actually had vampires in your village?" Amy asked.

Jamie shook his head. "C'mon, that stuff is just an old wives' tale."

"Maybe so, little one," Mrs. Romanoff replied, "but there is an old proverb which says, often from the waters of superstition arises the wispy mist of truth. I have lived a long time and seen enough to know this is true. Here in America people laugh at the old tales, but those of us from the old countries know better. Many peasant people in my village still hang whitehorn on their windows."

"I thought it was garlic that gave vampires the whammy," Jamie said jokingly.

Mrs. Romanoff nodded. "Yes, garlic, onions, leeks, and many herbs."

"That sounds more like our soup," said Amy. "Do these things really kill vampires?"

"To kill a vampire is very hard," explained the housekeeper. "These things only make them sick. But an old woman in my village with many special powers was said to drive nails through the heads of their corpses."

"That's gross," said Jamie.

"It is more horrible to be undead," Mrs. Romanoff said. "No one is safe from the vampire. If you lock yourself up in your house, you aren't safe. The vampire can come through chimneys and keyholes. My grandmother always rubbed all the keyholes with garlic—and the farm animals too. She had great knowledge of the vampire, but the family kept it secret. If a vampire knows you have discovered its identity, you are in much danger." Mrs. Romanoff went to the stove and carried the soup pot to the kitchen table. "It is important to weed them out," she continued, ladling soup into the children's bowls. "If a vampire goes undiscovered for seven years, it can travel to another country and become human again. It can even marry and have children, but all its children will become vampires—and all of them are born with teeth."

"I'd love to see a baby picture of Dr. Manheim," Amy whispered. "I'll bet he had a full set of choppers!"

"Why do you wish to write of such things?" she asked worriedly. "It is best not even to speak of such things. No one can be sure when the vampire is among us. To many people he seems normal as you or me. Only those of us with the old-world knowledge can see them for what they are."

Amy stared at her brother with "I told you so" written across her face. "You mean vampires can be lawyers or doctors?"

"Some say they may be anything by day, little one. Some also think the vampire only appears at night, but this isn't so. Sunlight hurts their eyes, but they are still very powerful. They have such strength, they can move with great speed and seem to disappear into thin air."

Jamie remembered how quickly Dr. Manheim had disappeared after stealing the diary—and how much he had been frightened by the sunlight. "Listen, this conversation is crazy; let's have lunch."

"I agree," said Mrs. Romanoff, sprinkling salt into the soup. "You children think of something nice to write about. Forget this awful business, yes? I am an old woman with old ideas and maybe they are crazy ones. Maybe. Since I come to this country, I think no more of vampires."

"And I'll think no more of them either," said Jamie.

He was anxious to put the entire subject behind him. But a question gnawed at the back of his mind:

If Dr. Manheim was not a vampire, then what the heck was going on?

It was definitely time to make contact with Jebediah Tredwell again!

Chapter Ten

THE HOUSE WAS UNUSUALLY QUIET. BEFORE MRS. ROMANoff had gone, she had put everything in typically tidy order. A pot of stew had been left to simmer on the stove, and freshly baked biscuits were keeping warm in the oven.

But the twins weren't hungry. For Jamie, a loss of appetite signified a troubled mind. In the past concrete facts had always led to inevitable conclusions, and logical reasoning had led to sensible deductions. But not this time.

Still, Jamie refused to believe Monroe had been invaded by ghouls and vampires, not even if it seemed that he had witnessed the fact with his own eyes. Sometimes what a person sees can merely be an illusion, he reasoned.

"Things may appear weird, Amy, but that's only because we don't have all the facts yet."

"I don't see what more Jebediah can tell us."

"I'm sure Dr. Manheim is involved in some experiment," Jamie said. "Maybe my hair-restoring idea was a flop, but I still think—"

"Come off it, Jamie. What experiment involves dead people and bloodsucking bats? That old man has turned the Brewster place into a house of horrors. I'm never going back there."

"Me either," he said, finally agreeing with his sister. "Just a few more clues and I'll figure this out. Please try to conjure up Jeb again. There must be something he hasn't told us."

"Okay, I'll try." Amy went to the china cabinet and took out the Paul Revere candlesticks, then she lit the candles and placed them on the coffee table.

"Must you do that hocus-pocus stuff first?" he asked. "Can't you just shout out his name?"

Amy grew impatient. Her brother refused to accept that she had no idea how her psychic powers worked. "I've told you, sometimes I think of Jeb and he doesn't come. Then the other night he just popped up in the pantry. I can't control this psychic stuff too well, so if candlesticks help me concentrate . . ."

"Okay, but it makes me feel like I'm at a séance or something."

"We'd better switch off the lights," Amy said. "I think Jeb prefers the dark."

The twins sat together on the sofa, then Amy closed her eyes and concentrated on Jebediah Tredwell. She envisioned him wandering across the lawn, in the area that had once been his beloved apple orchard. "We need to speak with you, Jeb," she whispered. "We're in big trouble here and Jamie made things worse. He insisted we go to the Brewster house last night and saw—"

"Don't blab all that junk," Jamie interrupted.

Amy opened her eyes and stared at her brother. "I'll tell Jeb whatever I like. Now you've made me lose my concentration." Closing her eyes again, she continued. "Please appear, Jeb. We need your help badly."

Presently the twins heard a knock at the front door.

"Old J.T. is getting awfully formal," said Jamie. "I never heard of a ghost who knocked. I'll let him in." Going to the door, Jamie half hoped that perhaps this time he would actually *see* his ancestral spirit.

What he saw was something far more startling than a friendly ghost.

Standing in the doorway was Dr. Manheim, but he was not alone. Beside him was the dead man Jamie had discovered the night before . . . only now he did not look quite as dead as he had then. The tall bald man was still very pale, and his eyes were glazed over as if he were in a trance. His body, though, seemed less rigid.

"Dr. Manheim! What are you doing here?"

Without waiting to be invited inside, the doctor entered the house. The ghastly half-dead creature followed him in silence.

The doctor smiled when he noticed Amy seated in a room lit only by candlelight. "You children prefer the darkness, just as I do? Perhaps you're truly children of the night, then? Forgive my intrusion, but I came to return something." He extended a gloved hand; in it he held Jamie's gold watch.

"Where'd you find that?" Jamie asked.

Amy knew the answer. Jamie had obviously dropped it when they had escaped from the Brewster house the night before—which meant Dr. Manheim knew they'd been snooping. Mrs. Romanoff's warning now seemed prophetic: "If a vampire knows you have discovered its identity, you are in much danger."

What would Manheim do? Amy wondered. And why had he brought the ghoulish zombie with him? She prayed Jebediah would materialize. Would a ghost be an equal match for a ghoul? She hoped so!

Dr. Manheim's voice had a distinctly sinister tone. "You're such a clever lad, I'm sure you must know where I found your watch."

Jamie stared at the doctor, then at his companion whose face showed no expression. The boy tried to remain calm. "I guess I dropped it at your house the other day. Thanks for returning it."

The emotional side of Jamie told him to run like lightning. Yet the sensible side (at least the side he chose to think of as sensible) still kept insisting there was a logical explanation for everything. After all, dead men don't get up and walk—not unless they're actually *undead*.

"I'm happy to return the watch," said the doctor. "Such a valuable timepiece would be much missed, I'm sure. But I can't think how it found its way into Frederick's bedroom." Dr. Manheim graciously gestured toward the dead man. "Allow me to introduce Frederick, my manservant."

90

Jamie backed away, then hurried to the sofa and sat down next to his sister. "Hi there," he said, forcing a note of brightness into his voice.

The dead man glanced toward the children, nodded stiffly, but said nothing.

"You must forgive Frederick's silence; he knows no English," the doctor explained.

Jamie tried to keep his hands from shaking. "There's not much point in his learning now," he mumbled.

"We should've saved some of that soup," Amy whispered. The ingredients in Mrs. Romanoff's recipe might have provided them with some protection against vampires, but they had eaten it all.

The candlelight cast sinister shadows across Dr. Manheim's face. "My reason for coming here is twofold. I'd like you children to join me for dessert."

"Thanks a lot," said Amy, "but it's awfully late."

"It's never too late for dessert," the doctor said firmly.

"We're not very hungry," Jamie said.

"Perhaps not for food, but I perceive you have a great hunger for information. You're both such bright, clever children," he said menacingly, "I suspect you've already uncovered my little secret."

"No, we haven't," Jamie said.

"I'm not at all clever," Amy protested.

"That's right," Jamie agreed. "Ask anyone. They'll tell you my sister is *stupid*."

"Foolhardy, perhaps, but surely not stupid. Yet you fail to realize that every new discovery presents an element of danger. When you made your uninvited entry into my home, you may have opened up Pandora's box, so to speak. Nevertheless, initiative shouldn't go unrewarded. Perhaps when you understand the circumstances fully, you'll be disposed to keep my little secret.'' Dr. Manheim wrapped his cape across his shoulders, then gestured toward the door. "Shall we go?"

"Go where?" Jamie asked.

"To my house, naturally. This time you'll have no need to sneak inside, for this time you are my guests. Frederick shall be your chaperon. He has agreed to see that you both return safely home."

Frederick nodded with a grunt, then approached the children. The twins stared up at the bald dead man and realized they had little choice. The doctor had made them an offer they couldn't refuse!

Jamie nudged his sister. "Where's Jeb when we need him?" he mumbled.

"I don't know," she whispered, "but if he doesn't come soon, it'll be too late!"

Chapter Eleven

SOLEMNLY THE TWINS WALKED OUT THE DOOR. DR. MANHEIM preceded them, and Frederick followed close behind.

Amy knew it was pointless to try to escape from a zombie and a vampire, but she kept hoping someone would notice them as they walked through town. Unfortunately, the streets of Monroe were deserted.

As they approached the woods Dr. Manheim sucked in a deep breath of the cold air. "Don't you find the night invigorating?"

The twins found the night air bone-chillingly cold and the woods dark as pitch.

"I wish we had a flashlight," Jamie said.

"No need," said the doctor, "I see quite well in the dark. Just a little farther and all your questions will be answered."

Amy dug her nails into her brother's wrist. "I didn't

93

want any answers," she grumbled. "*You* were the one, smarty. If only you'd listened to me—"

"Let's not argue," Jamie said. "*We're* all we've got."

Trudging their way through the darkness, Amy tried to envision what awaited them. Was it death? All she saw in her mind's eye was continued darkness. Surely, death was more than that. Jebediah was proof. He'd been dead more than two hundred years, yet his spirit still existed. Or did it? she wondered. Was it possible the lieutenant colonel's ghostly visits were actually products of her imagination? Why didn't he appear now when she needed him so desperately?

Dr. Manheim approached the clearing in the woods. "Here we are."

In the moonlight the Brewster house loomed dark and ominous. A woman stood at the entrance. As they approached her Amy saw that she was the woman they'd seen wandering through the graveyard. Jamie noticed she was still carrying the small metal box in her hand.

"This is my niece, Illona," Dr. Manheim explained. "Have you been out walking, my dear?"

The woman nodded, then turned to enter the house, never once acknowledging the twins' presence.

"Please forgive Illona for not greeting you. You see, my niece is blind. I've equipped her with the metal apparatus which makes it possible for her to get around unattended. At present it's quite a primitive invention but a uniquely simple idea. It's based on the principle of echo location."

Jamie watched as the woman entered the living room. As she approached the sofa, she began singing a high note. It was the same plaintive cry that the children had heard the night before in the cemetery. As if in response, the box emitted a high-frequency signal. Hearing it, she moved aside to avoid bumping into the sofa.

Jamie was so fascinated, he suddenly forgot that they faced danger. "How's that thing work?"

Dr. Manheim seemed eager to explain. "It replicates the natural sonar found in porpoises, dolphins, and bats. As you may know, *sonar* is a contraction of the phrase '*so*und *na*vigation *r*anging.' Vision being impractical in the sea, porpoises orient themselves by listening to the reflected echoes of their own noises."

The logical explanation Jamie had been searching for seemed to be at hand. "So that's why you keep bats!"

Dr. Manheim looked surprised. "You know about my bats as well? You are exceptionally clever children. It seems another of my little secrets has been discovered. I'm sure you realize the reason I did not advertise the presence of bats in my home. Some people might find it disturbing to have such creatures close by, but their presence here is essential."

"Part of your secret project, right?" Jamie asked eagerly.

"Exactly. As I explained, both porpoises and bats have the unique ability of echo location. Needless to say, one can only study porpoises underwater, but no such problem arises with the study of an air-dwelling animal. The mere size and weight of a porpoise make it impossible to maintain it in a laboratory, but large numbers of experimental bats can be stored in a hibernating state in refrigerated containers. When I require them for research, I simply thaw them out."

95

"I get it," said Jamie. "Your niece hears the sound of her own voice echoing back from that metal box and she can *hear* where she's going."

"Precisely. The apparatus is still in a primitive stage, but I soon hope to perfect it. I was fortunate to find this house adjoining the cemetery; Illona can wander here at will without putting herself in physical danger."

"I see your point," said Jamie. "I guess you wouldn't want her trying it out in traffic."

Reaching the sofa, Illona sat down, placing the box beside her. "You didn't tell me you were bringing guests, Uncle Gustav."

"These are Professor Ferguson's children, my dear. Their names are Amy and Jamie. You were out practicing with your machine the day they came to visit."

Illona stared blankly and nodded. "I'm happy to meet you both." She called to Frederick and spoke to him in German. "I've asked our manservant to prepare us all some tea."

Frederick grunted, then slowly entered the kitchen.

Illona smiled. "How nice to have visitors. Uncle Gustav so rarely has visitors. Perhaps Frederick will find some cookies in the pantry as well."

Amy didn't want a cookie—she wanted to go home. Maybe Jamie bought all that garbage about echo location, but she didn't. She was still convinced she was in the presence of two vampires and one zombie!

A clattering sound came from the kitchen, followed by a crash of dishes. Illona turned toward the sound. "Poor Frederick. Is he having another attack, Uncle?"

Dr. Manheim glanced toward the door. "There's no cause for concern," he replied. "Frederick merely dropped some dishes."

Illona sighed. "Poor Frederick is subject to such dreadful attacks. Uncle Gustav has been trying to help him for years."

Dr. Manheim sat next to his niece, stroking her hand sympathetically. "And I shall continue to do so, my dear. My experiments into catalepsy are finally showing results. Someday soon Frederick may be free from these terrible attacks."

Jamie was more fascinated than ever. "Catalepsy? Isn't that some sort of sleeping sickness?"

"Quite right," said the doctor. "As yet science knows little of its origin. Often a deep sleep comes upon the victim, and it may last for hours, weeks, or days. The pulse and respiration slow and the body becomes cold. During a severe attack respiration may become so feeble that death is simulated. In the past many people with this ailment were buried alive. Can you imagine the horror of waking up in a coffin, realizing you've been buried by mistake? Such horrors bring to mind the tales of Edgar Allan Poe. I know a case of a man in Leipzig who so feared premature burial, he placed a clause in his will stipulating that he be buried with a bell. If he awoke in his coffin, he hoped to summon help with the sound."

Illona grew upset. "Poor Frederick," she said, close to tears.

"Don't worry, my child, this will never happen to our dear friend. I've placed a lock on his door to insure that he does not wander off when he's in one of his trancelike states."

Jamie moved to one of the overstuffed chairs. He relaxed and crossed his legs. "What do you know, everything is finally beginning to make *perfect sense*."

"I'm glad you think so." The doctor smiled.

Amy found his smile decidedly sneaky and definitely suspicious!

Frederick emerged from the kitchen. In robotlike fashion he placed a tea tray on the table, then moved to a corner and sat there in stony silence.

Jamie's appetite had finally returned. He reached for a cookie. It felt hard, looked stale, and smelled slightly like a basement, but he ate it anyway. "For a while we thought something odd was going on out here," he confessed. "At least Amy did. But I told her she was crazy. Amy has an overactive imagination."

"Indeed?" the doctor said. "I suspected as much. But people like yourself with logical, scientific minds can always unearth a reasonable explanation for things."

"Right," Jamie said smugly, and gobbled down another cookie. "That's what I'm always telling my sister, but she never listens."

Amy glared at her brother. His predictably pompous know-it-all attitude was feeding right into Dr. Manheim's plans. Jamie was now a helpless fly caught in the doctor's web of flattery and deceit.

"Now that everything is explained," said the doctor, "I'm sure you children can put aside your suspicions."

"You haven't explained everything," said Amy boldly. Common sense told her not to ask any questions, but

Jamie's smugness had provoked her. "If *all* bats have echo location, why do you keep *vampire* bats?"

Dr. Manheim looked startled but quickly regained his composure. "You children know more than I suspected. How did you come by that knowledge?"

"My favorite horse at Briarcliff Stables was attacked by a vampire bat," she replied coldly.

"Yes, that was most unfortunate. Occasionally one of my specimens gets loose despite my precautions. To answer your question, you could say I was attempting to kill two birds with one stone, so to speak. I'm working on two experiments involving bats, and one requires the vampire variety. At present I'm attempting to find a cure for fatal thrombosis, blood clots that can prove deadly. I'm hoping to create a serum from the saliva of vampire bats that would destroy such blood clots in the human body. The wound of a vampire bat contains an anticoagulant ingredient that prevents the blood from clotting immediately. Once I isolate that ingredient, a serum may be produced that could save many lives."

Amy did not believe that the sinister old man was actually a dedicated healer.

Jamie, however, seemed totally impressed. "You're sure involved in some fascinating experiments," he said. "If you ever need an assistant while you're in Monroe, I'd really be interested."

"I'll seriously consider that offer," replied the doctor, smiling.

Jamie winced. Dr. Manheim's teeth seemed unusually long and sharp. Why hadn't he noticed that before? Jamie gulped down the remnant of the cookie that had lodged in his throat. It was only then that he noticed its distinctly medicinal taste.

"Now that I've explained everything to your satisfaction," Dr. Manheim went on, "I'm sure you'll understand my continued need for privacy. It's imperative that I continue my experiments in seclusion, so I trust you'll keep my little secrets."

Jamie felt himself getting slightly drowsy, but there was still an important question he hadn't asked. "Why'd you steal Alexander Cartwright's diary from Hillcrest?"

"You're certainly perceptive," said the old man, stiffening with anger. "How did you discover that fact?"

"I saw you from the school window," Jamie explained. "I suppose the diary mentioned something about your secret experiments, right?"

"What a truly clever young man you are, Jamie. Yes, that's it, of course. Alexander Cartwright's diary unknowingly reveals many sensitive aspects of my most secret experiment. It's a project members of my family have been working on for more than two hundred years. I hope to find a cure for a grave physical disorder, of which many of my ancestors were victims. Sadly, I'm also afflicted with this genetic disorder. I never speak of it, for it is a disease that strikes fear in the hearts of many. Please understand that what I reveal to you is in the strictest confidence. I am a victim of porphyria."

The twins stared at each other. Neither of them had heard the word before. "What's that?" Jamie asked.

"It's a rare genetic disorder," the doctor explained. "It

involves malfunctioning in the body's manufacture of crucial chemicals. Exposure to even mild sunlight can disfigure the skin. This is why I prefer to venture forth at night. Certain foods, such as garlic, aggravate this chemical imbalance."

"Don't say any more, Uncle Gustav," Illona said anxiously. "You mustn't reveal our family secrets."

"Calm yourself, my dear. These children's suspicions are already aroused, so I must confess my indiscretions. It was wrong of me to steal the diary, but I had to protect my experiment. Certain facts were revealed in those pages that mustn't be publicized as yet."

Jamie yawned. Why had he suddenly grown so tired? "What facts?" he said.

"Certain delicate matters," the doctor explained. "Nature has attempted to help the porphyria victim compensate for this photosensitivity. Many sufferers of the disease become quite hairy, and this is the reason why I always wear gloves. My ancestor Heinrich Manheim suffered a similar indignity. Then, of course, there is the ever-present desire for *fresh blood*."

Amy shuddered. To calm herself, she took a sip of tea. It had already turned cold and had a moldy undertaste. She pushed the cup aside, feeling dizzy.

"Please, Uncle Gustav," begged Illona, "you mustn't say any more."

"The truth has been revealed, my dear; we cannot change that fact." Dr. Manheim glanced at the twins with a solemn expression. "Naturally, this blood lust is assuaged by eating rare meats. Perhaps in previous generations my ancestors were not quite so humanitarian. I daresay many people may have considered them to be—"

"Vampires?" Amy interrupted.

Dr. Manheim cringed. *"Unusual,"* he said, correcting her. "After all, folklore and superstition are merely based on ignorance. In any event, to compensate for the theft of the diary, I'm prepared to give over all my research notes to the town of Monroe once my experiments are published. This should be ample retribution, don't you agree?"

Jamie's hunger for logic was now totally satisfied. Everything made sense. The mystery surrounding Dr. Manheim was solved, and all his experiments fit into neat, tidy little boxes . . .

Neat, tidy little boxes, he repeated as furniture and faces began to rotate before his eyes. They moved slowly at first, then faster and faster . . . faster and faster, until he felt himself caught in a whirlpool.

Amy wanted desperately to believe Dr. Manheim's explanation, but she couldn't. The psychic part of her mind still kept conjuring up frightening images. She envisioned huge crates of earth hidden directly below them in the basement . . . a hugh crate of sacred ground in which Dr. Manheim slept after his nocturnal wanderings. Crates of earth in which all his ancestors from the past had slept . . . all his relatives of the present still slept. Gustav Manheim, Illona Manheim, Heinrich Manheim. The dizzying image spun around in her head, over and over again. She closed her eyes, desperately hoping the vision would cease. When she reopened them, the room grew fuzzy, as if she were viewing it through a gauzy filter.

The figures were gone from the room now, replaced by three bats with giant wings. Three vampire bats with long, sharp, bloodied teeth hovered over Jamie's body, making horrid screeching noises.

Amy felt too weak and dizzy to scream. Her eyelids seemed as heavy as lead, yet she tried to keep them open. Was that really Jamie she saw, asleep and lifeless in the chair? No, he mustn't sleep. They must escape—escape their horrible, inevitable fate. But how? Her legs refused to move. It was as if every part of her body belonged to someone else and she no longer had control. Darkness and evil now had control. And the power of that evil was sapping the remaining strength from her body. Still, she refused to give in to that power, sensing there was a far greater strength in the universe than evil. *Goodness* was that greater power.

Then in the doorway, she saw the light. It was a brilliantly white light: a pure light consisting of myriad particles that suddenly fused into a familiar shape.

"Jebediah!" Amy gasped, and reached out her hand. "You've come at last."

The light emanating from Jebediah's spirit became almost blinding. As it radiated through the room, the three bats screeched hysterically and cringed in the corner; then, with a noisy flutter of wings, they escaped through the window.

Her body still weak and her head spinning, Amy felt Jebediah's spirit move closer. There had been rage and indignation in his eyes when he cast the creatures from the room, but now there was only consolation. "You and

103

your brother have proved yourselves to be quite reckless," he chided, "so it is incumbent upon me to make that observation. Still, I am pledged to exert whatever ability I am possessed of in your favor, therefore I cannot in justice do otherwise. But I must charge you, child, never to enter this house again. I feel nothing but the utmost horror and detestation for the forces which live within these walls." As Jebediah extended his hand, a glowing force emanated from his fingertips. "Rise now, child, and begone."

"I can't move," she protested. "Dr. Manheim must've drugged us."

"You must find the strength to do so," Jeb said. "My astral emanation will help you in this endeavor. Rise, Cousin, and give aid to your brother."

Amy suddenly felt the strength returning to her limbs. Staggering across the room, she began to shake Jamie back into consciousness.

"My spirit force shall guide you through the woods," Jebediah assured her. "But my power to come to your aid in a like fashion again is severely limited. List now but one thing more, and I must be gone. You must entreat the aid of one who knows the ancient folklore. She alone may help you find the direct road to the attainment of your wishes."

"Do you mean Mrs. Romanoff?" Amy asked.

Jebediah nodded. "Inquire of her the particulars of a need-fire ceremony. This and this alone will return safety to your household."

Before Amy could ask anything more, Jebediah's presence had faded from sight.

Jamie didn't bother to take his uniform over his jeans.
"You made the same mistake."
"You were pretending, too?" Amy asked. "I thought
I was the—"

Chapter Twelve

WHEN JAMIE AWOKE THE NEXT MORNING, HIS HEAD FELT LIKE
a large watermelon that had been used in football practice! The events of the night before seemed fuzzy. Glancing under the covers, he saw that he was still wearing his
jeans and sweatshirt. Why hadn't he changed into paja-
mas? he wondered.

He got out of bed and knocked on his sister's door.
Amy was still in bed but was wide awake. "What went
on last night?" he asked. "Last thing I remember, I was
having this fascinating conversation with Dr. Manheim,
then all of a sudden I woke up—with all my clothes on."

"I'll tell you what happened," she shouted. "We were
nearly *murdered*. Dr. Manheim drugged us, then all three of
those weirdos turned into bats and were about to suck our
blood. Luckily, Jeb materialized and frightened them away.
He projected his astral energy to help us get home safely."

Jamie didn't bother to hide his skepticism. "Go back to sleep, you need lots more rest!"

"Don't you remember any of it?" she asked. "It's true, I swear it."

"Sure, it sounds real likely. Honestly, Amy, you never give up, do you? Dr. Manheim gave us a logical explanation for everything, so why make up a cockamamy story like that?"

"What do *you* think happened last night?"

"Well, I guess we got tired, so Bald Freddy escorted us home."

"Then why can't you remember?"

"Like I said, I was tired."

"Drugged."

Jamie considered that possibility. "Well, those cookies did taste strange." He walked toward the door. "Hold it, I'll be right back." He returned with the dictionary and leafed through the *p*'s. "Here it is," he said smugly. " 'Porphyria: photosensitivity and hepatic dysfunction.' See, it's right here in black and white."

"What's that prove?" Amy said. "I'll bet the word *vampire* is in that dictionary too. And the word *liar*. And the word *stupid!*"

"How about the word *crazy*? Dr. Manheim is a dedicated scientist, just like he told us."

Disgusted by Jamie's stubbornness, Amy punched her pillow. If only her brother could *remember*. If he had been conscious, he would have seen with his own eyes how Dr. Manheim turned into a bat!

Jamie's skepticism suddenly made Amy doubt her own

memory. Had the sight actually been some horrible nightmare? Had Jeb really saved them from death, or had it been a hysterical illusion? Amy could not be certain. Then she remembered Jeb's parting words. "Okay," she said, "maybe you're right. But what if you're wrong? If Dr. Manheim stays in Monroe, everyone might wind up with puncture marks on their necks, just like Bluebell!"

Jamie's head began to throb. He certainly felt as if he had been drugged. Why couldn't he remember how they had gotten home? "Okay, I admit I don't know which of us is right. So what'll we do about it?"

"We'll take Jebediah's advice and speak to Mrs. Romanoff right away."

The twins weren't certain how to broach such a delicate subject, since their conversation the day before had obviously upset Mrs. Romanoff. They followed her around the house as she went about her chores. Then Amy watched as the old woman brewed the afternoon tea, which was made with camomile from the garden. "I'll help," she said, stirring the pot.

"No, little one," Mrs. Romanoff cautioned, "don't stir it widdershins. This invites the power of darkness." She observed the twins' puzzled expression. "A silly superstition, I know, but to be careful doesn't hurt. Some say to stir a pot from right to left can cause much trouble." She took the pot from Amy and poured them both a cup of sweet-smelling tea. "Is good for your colds, yes?"

Amy nodded. "Speaking of superstition, Jamie and I—"

107

"I will speak of them no more," the woman interrupted. "I don't wish to frighten you with such thoughts."

"We're not frightened," Amy said. "We'd like to hear more."

"You wish to put such things in your story?"

"That's right," Amy said. "Could you tell us something about a need-fire ceremony?"

"Where did you hear of such things?" Mrs. Romanoff asked.

"From an old friend," Jamie interjected. "A *really* old friend."

Mrs. Romanoff poured herself some tea and took a seat beside the twins. "I remember such a ceremony in my village when I was very little. A need-fire is a form of purification to combat vampires and other evil spirits. It is very powerful."

"How's it work?" asked Jamie. "Is it like burning a vampire at the stake, or what?"

"No, the vampire need not be present at the ceremony. If he is nearby, the need-fire will drive him away from the place. But the fire cannot be started by a match. Friction is the only way."

"I get it," Jamie said. "You'd have to rub sticks together like the Boy Scouts do, right?"

Mrs. Romanoff nodded. "This is exactly so. Once the flame has started, you must light a piece of cloth. Then you use the cloth to light the bonfire."

"That doesn't sound too hard," said Amy.

"But the ceremony must be carried out at night," the housekeeper continued, "without artificial light. If man-made light appears, the need-fire will not perform the purification. The old magic will die."

"Not even a flashlight?" asked Jamie, quickly seeing the difficulty involved in such a ceremony.

"No light at all," said Mrs. Romanoff, "only the moon. You must pick a night when the moon is full. When I was young, we did this in my village and all the sick animals grew well. The evil spirits left their bodies never to return."

"There's supposed to be a full moon on Halloween," Amy whispered. "Maybe we could—"

"Come off it," Jamie snapped. "How can we start a *bonfire* in the middle of Monroe? We'd be arrested by the fire department. They've got laws against stuff like that."

The steady thumping sound from the washing machine stopped, and Mrs. Romanoff went into the pantry to put the laundry into the dryer.

"Maybe we could get special permission to start a fire," Amy said.

"How? Should we tell the fire chief we need to scare away some vampires?"

"We must do something," Amy said. "We can't pass up that full moon. Halloween would be the perfect time to have the ceremony. Maybe we could sneak into the park and burn some branches. If we're lucky, no one will find out about it."

Jamie thought a moment, then got what he considered to be a brilliant idea. "You're right, but with any luck, *everyone* will know about it. In fact, the whole town will be there!"

*   *   *

"How'd you ever think of such a great idea?" asked Mr. Ferguson over dessert that night.

"I guess I was inspired," Jamie said proudly.

His father agreed. "It'll make it the best Halloween celebration this town has ever had. Are you sure you've checked everything out with Larry MacDermott?"

"Sure, Dad. The fire chief said his own kids love the idea of an old-fashioned bonfire in the park. Naturally, we'll need a permit, but he's arranging for that. And I made all the other arrangements. I called tons of people who all agreed to bring their dead branches to Winchester Field on Halloween."

"It sounds rather like Guy Fawkes Day," said Mr. Ferguson, always eager to interject a historical fact into a conversation. "In England every November fifth they set bonfires and burn effigies to commemorate the thwarted effort to blow up the houses of Parliament in 1605." He turned toward his wife. "What do you think of Jamie's plan, Miriam? Isn't it terrific?"

Miriam Ferguson had ignored her dessert. "What's that, Richard? I didn't hear you," she said, busily writing down a long list of items. "Why do you suppose your aunt needs three blenders, six metal file cabinets, two weather vanes, and four stereo speakers?"

"Is that what eccentric Aunt Edith bought yesterday?" Amy asked.

"That's only part of it," her mother said. "She also bought three plush teddy bears and a set of electric trains.

You don't suppose Aunt Edith has become senile, do you, Richard?"

"I doubt it. The world encompasses many peculiar people, Miriam, but I think there's room for us all."

Not quite all, Amy hoped. There shouldn't be room for *evil* people—at least not in Monroe.

With any luck, after the Halloween ceremony three of them would be gone!

Chapter Thirteen

By dusk on Friday, October thirty-first, a gruesome band of monsters, goblins, witches, and various other horrifying creatures had assembled in Winchester Field.

Children in fantastic costumes, their faces painted garishly, or concealed by grotesque masks, ran around the oak and maple trees, menacing one another. Many parents and relatives had also come in appropriately frightening attire. Even Miss Apthorp was wearing a large papier-mâché mask that the third-grade art class had created especially for her.

"I'm not certain if it's a lizard or a dragon," she explained. "But it's definitely difficult to see through it," she added, and nearly bumped into a bench.

For several hours the townspeople of Monroe had been gathering. For hours as well members of the community had been piling fallen tree branches, broken boughs, and loose kindling wood into a pyramid shape, to prepare for the upcoming bonfire.

Mrs. Eliot had selected David Toshito's story as the very finest entry in her contest. David was to read it aloud during the celebration. Amy had totally ignored the assignment, and Jamie had been far too busy with arrangements for the evening to complete his Green Mold Monster epic. But he took comfort in the knowledge that if he had had the time to finish, he certainly would have won.

At the moment he had more important business at hand. That morning Jamie had busily brushed up on his Boy Scout training, to make certain he had not forgotten how to create a friction fire. He prepared a twelve-inch piece of elmwood, rounded one end, then tapered the other to make a spindle. With various other pieces of hardwood, he created a hand piece and the all-important fire board. With the branches and wood tucked safely in his pocket, Jamie now eagerly awaited nightfall.

As did everyone else. Witches, large and small, skittered across the grass on broomsticks. Melissa Petronio wore her black cat costume which her mother had made for the school play the year before. Nelson Rappaport had borrowed his sister's high-heeled boots, which made him a convincingly tall Frankenstein's monster, complete with bolts attached to his neck. There were several vampires wearing black felt capes and long bloody false teeth, terrorizing whoever passed by.

"Where's your costume, Amy?" asked Sarah Richardson. (Sarah was Amy's least favorite person in the entire world.) She had come dressed as a witch, which Amy considered highly appropriate and perfect typecasting.

The twins had not had time to create costumes, but Amy had managed to unearth two bat masks in the basement. She slipped hers on, then stuck her tongue out through the mouth hole. "Buzz off, Sarah, before I bite your throat."

"How utterly juvenile," Sarah said haughtily. She adjusted her steeple-crowned hat and walked off to join two mummies and a young man who looked like a slice of bread but was, he explained, a tombstone.

Despite the outward frivolity of the evening, Amy was fully aware of the seriousness of the mission she and Jamie had undertaken. While children romped about in their vampire costumes, she knew that real ones were close by.

"I still don't buy your cockeyed theory," Jamie said, watching people stack more branches onto the pile. "But if there's any truth in it, this plan can't hurt—especially since everyone loves the idea."

As October's last hours slowly drew to a close, a full moon became visible in the evening sky. The park sank into darkness as a single cloud floated ominously across the moon, and a chilling autumn wind swept through the trees. Amy felt as if icy, shadowy fingers were grasping her from behind, stirring up all her fears of the unseen and unknown. The powers of darkness had taken control.

Jamie glanced over the crowd. The figures huddled around the pyramid of branches seemed to have taken on a strangely menacing appearance. They looked no longer

114

like children masquerading as monsters but more like true demons, summoned up from some evil lower depth.

Almost in unison the crowd began chanting, "The fire, the fire, let's start the fire!"

Mr. Ferguson was seated beside Larry MacDermott. "You'd better get this show on the road, Larry," he observed. "I think the natives are restless."

The fire chief stood up, taking a lighter from his pocket. "Okay, kids, are you ready?"

As the children let out squeals of delight, Jamie rushed over and grabbed the lighter from Larry MacDermott. "I've a better idea," he said. "Let's show the kids how the Boy Scouts do it."

Jamie threw some tinder on the ground, knelt down, and placed his fire board above it, steadying it with one foot. He twisted the bowstring he had made around his carved branch spindle, pressing down the hand piece on top of the spindle to keep it steady. With long even strokes of the bow, he set the spindle spinning until a heavy smoke began to produce a glowing ember. Then Jamie blew on it until the tinder underneath gradually turned into a fire.

When the fire had taken hold, Amy handed him an old towel which he ignited in the flame. Grabbing a branch from the pile, Jamie placed the flaming towel onto it, then held it above his head dramatically. "We call upon the powers of darkness to be gone," he shouted. Hurling the burning cloth onto the pyramid, he set the branches ablaze.

Cheers and applause swelled up from the crowd as the

wood crackled and became enveloped with flames. Adults in the crowd made certain the children kept a safe distance from the blaze. Then Mrs. Eliot asked David Toshito to read his prizewinning story.

David cleared his throat nervously. Light from the blazing bonfire flickered around his face as he began: " 'The Dismembered Head,' " he said solemnly. " 'There was once a beautiful young woman named Miko who lived in a golden pavilion overlooking the mountains. Each morning she would glance at her lovely image in the waters of Lake Chuzenji, to thank the spirit gods for her great beauty. But in the waters of Lake Chuzenji there lived five demons who envied Miko's loveliness. One day . . .' "

The children of Monroe sat huddled around the bonfire totally engrossed in David's tale of ghosts and demons. The twins, however, sat in silence, totally engrossed in their own private thoughts.

Would the need-fire ceremony work? Amy wondered. Would it purify the town of Monroe and cast out the three terrifying vampires?

Had all this hocus-pocus been necessary? Jamie wondered. Or had Dr. Manheim been telling the truth all along?

Only time would tell.

" '. . . Miko gazed into the rippling water,' " David continued, " 'but she did not see the image of her great beauty. Instead, she saw a horrifying sight. . . .' "

Little children gasped from underneath their frightening masks and clutched their parents' hands as David proceeded with his story. Vampires of various sizes and shapes wrapped their capes around them to keep out the cold.

Three shadowy figures stood at a slight distance from the rest of the crowd. They slowly began to move to one side. Amy noticed them immediately. They were all wearing long capes, and one of them was a woman with long flowing hair. As the moonlight caught them in silhouette, they wrapped their capes about them like giant wings. Almost instantly the large black wings were transformed into smaller wings. The three small creatures flew toward the bonfire, hovered about it screeching, then flew away.

The fire chief blinked. "What the heck was that?" he asked.

"Night owls, I guess," said Richard Ferguson. "What else?"

Amy knew what else they might be; indeed, what else they *were*.

In a silent prayer she asked that by morning the evil infecting Monroe be gone.

Chapter Fourteen

EXHAUSTED BY THE EVENTS OF THE NIGHT BEFORE, THE TWINS slept late the next morning. When they came down to breakfast, the sun was beaming through the kitchen window. Their parents were having coffee with Emilio Sanchez, a language professor from Monroe University.

As Amy sat down, she was startled to find a small *skull* resting on the breakfast plate. Jamie was equally startled to discover a little *skeleton* lying on his plate.

Professor Sanchez laughed. "They're made of spun sugar," he explained, "to celebrate día de muertos, the 'day of the dead.' In Mexico, November first is like your Halloween. We always give children these little spun-sugar objects to remind them that death is simply a passage from one world into another. I hope you don't find my gift too macabre."

Jamie broke off his skeleton's leg and stirred it into his

118

tea. "No, I like it, it's cute—in a macabre sort of way, of course."

"Richard told me about last night's bonfire," said the professor. "I'm sorry I missed it."

"It was a great event," said Mrs. Ferguson, "Monroe's best Halloween ever—and the scariest too. We even had some night owls join the ceremony."

"But now all the ghouls, goblins, and vampires have disappeared," said Mr. Ferguson, "at least until next year."

Amy prayed the real ones had disappeared forever, but she had to be certain. "I'd like to visit the Brewster place later," she said casually, "to remind Dr. Manheim he planned to come to dinner this weekend."

"He won't be coming," said her father. "Emilio just told me the strangest thing. Apparently Dr. Manheim left Monroe unexpectedly last night. The dean found a note in his office this morning. Manheim has canceled the remainder of his seminars."

"He also left a note for you, Richard," said Mr. Sanchez, handing it to him.

"Could you read it aloud, Dad?" asked Amy.

Mr. Ferguson opened the envelope and read the message:

"Dear Professor Ferguson,

"Powers beyond my control have forced me to return to Leipzig immediately. I had hoped my stay would be longer, but circumstances proved otherwise. I thank you for your hospitality. Please re-

119

member me to your children, both of whom have exhibited insight, intelligence, and determination.

"Knowing we shall never meet again, I remain
"Respectfully,
"Gustav Manheim."

"Well," said Mrs. Ferguson, "old Manheim is an odd bird. He thought highly of you children, though. Whatever project he's working on, he certainly kept it secret. I wonder what it could be."

Jamie sipped his orange juice in silence. What did it all mean? he wondered. Had he actually helped free Monroe from the horrid curse of vampires? More than likely, he had lost a possible chance to assist a brilliant scientist. In doing so, he may have let a potentially lucrative career fly out the window. He dunked the remainder of his sugared skeleton into his teacup, sullenly watching it dissolve into nothingness.

Amy sat in silence as well, but her feelings were decidedly different from her brother's. She sensed that a dark cloud had lifted from Monroe. Somewhere in her mind, far beyond ordinary knowledge, she knew the powers of light would always win out over the powers of darkness.

Her feeling was confirmed when Fred Weatherby phoned from Briarcliff Stables.

"Hi, Amy," he said, "I called to tell you Bluebell has finally recovered."

"Really? Are you sure she's okay now?"

"Better than ever. She was a sick mare, but she snapped back during the night. This morning she devoured her feed. I'm sure Bluebell would love a good ride today."

"I'll be right over," she said, then hung up.

Mrs. Ferguson poured her daughter some milk. "Drink this before you go. We have fresh milk again, now that Crowley's cows are back to normal."

As Amy glanced down at the glass, she received a mental picture of the two diaries Dr. Manheim had stolen. Amy knew he had returned them both before leaving. One was safely back in its place at the Historical Society, the other was resting in the display case at Hillcrest Academy.

"*Everything* is back to normal now, Mom," said Amy excitedly.

The phone rang again. This time it was for Jamie. The caller was Alan Hotchkiss, one of the mayor's aides. "I heard you staged quite a show over in Winchester Field last night, young man. How'd you like to make it an annual event? Celebrations like that are great for Monroe's self-image, you know. They keep the citizens happy."

The recognition was great for Jamie's self-image too. When he got off the phone, his mind began to see new career possibilities. "Maybe I could stage an event for *every* holiday. Who knows where a thing like this could lead? I might wind up the mayor myself someday!"

Amy laughed. "Like I said, everything is back to normal!"

Amy rode Bluebell through open fields brilliant with the reds and golds of the autumn leaves. One season had died, but another was beginning.

Amy grasped the mare's chestnut mane, remembering

what Professor Sanchez had said: "death is simply a passage from one world into another." Having met Jebediah Tredwell, she knew that was true. Amy had no idea when they might meet again, but the knowledge that Jeb's spirit existed somewhere made her feel safe, secure, and part of some infinite, universal plan.

Bluebell whinnied with pleasure, kicked up her hoofs, and together they raced toward the sunlight.